THE ISLAND AT THE END OF THE WORLD

Sam Taylor is the author of *The Republic of Trees* and *The Amnesiac*. He lives in France.

THE ISLAND AT THE END
OF THE WORLD

Sam Taylor

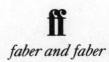

faber and faber

First published in 2009
by Faber and Faber Ltd
Bloomsbury House
74–77 Great Russell Street
London WC1B 3DA
This edition published in 2010

Typeset by RefineCatch Ltd, Bungay, Suffolk
Printed in the UK by CPI Bookmarque, Croydon
All rights reserved
© Sam Taylor, 2009

A CIP record for this book is available from the British Library

ISBN 978–0–571–24052–4

for Oscar, Milo and Paul-Emile

Contents

Part One

Part Two

PART ONE

And the waters decreased continually until the tenth month: in the tenth month, on the first day of the month, were the tops of the mountains seen.

Genesis 8 : 5

I

Hast thou found me, O mine enemy?

I don't know who you are but you're headed into trouble.

So, stranger, do yourself a favor. DO NOT COME ANY CLOSER TO THIS ISLAND. *Turn around now and go back where you came from.*

I have lived here with my children since the Great Flood seven springtimes ago, and we are happy here. Me and my family, we are UNCONTAMINATED.

You, O dark dot on my horizon, O mote in my telescopic sights, come from a God-damned place. You may have escaped drowning but you're still soiled and spoiled by the evils that stalked this land before the Great Wave crashed down and swallowed them all up. Like the angel said, Babylon is fallen, is fallen and is become the habitation of devils. And you, stranger, partook of her sins, you received her plagues, you are tainted by her poisons.

IF YOU COME ANY CLOSER I WILL KILL YOU I SWEAR.

You can't see me but I can see you. I have you in my crosshairs now. Turn around and sail back to your own island or believe me you're a deadman.

I put down the pen, breathing heavily, and read through what I've written. It's OK, I guess. It'll do. Truth is, it's hard to tell a stranger how much you hate them just by writing words on a piece of paper. I could make the point so much more eloquently with my eyeballs an inch from his and my hands round his throat.

But (relax, deep breaths) I don't want it to go that far, not if I can help it. The risks are too great. These words could save both of us from Hell, so I need to make them perfect. Right now, though, I'm still too angry to think clearly so I fold the paper up and slide it in the pocket of my fleece. Then I stand up from the desk and climb into my long rabbit-fur coat, walk outside, close and lock the door of the wooden cabin behind me, and begin the walk through the forest.

Springtime's late this year. Frost and ice reign unmelted in the shadows on the ground, where leaves crunch beneath my boots. The sky I see in shreds through the canopy of naked oak branches is the same low dead-ash grey it's been for months now, and the air's the same soul-sucking cold. But listen to me, I sound like a fickle woman, moaning about the horrors of winter. Lord, I am sorry for my weakness. I know without Your grace myself and my family would not even be alive now. You saved us from the fate the others suffered and I will always love and obey You, for You are the resurrection and the light, Amen.

I can feel the tendons in my legs tensing as I climb the slope. I haven't been out much lately, only to chop firewood and hunt. Mostly we've survived on soup and salted meat and spent our days in the ark, the four of us huddled near the woodburner. It's been good – the songs, the stories, the love – but I guess in those frozen months my body's rusted up, the skin thinned, muscles wasted, lungs shrivelled like week-old party balloons. Alice, Finn and Daisy are all fine because they're young, but at my age you need to keep the engine turning over. I won't let myself get so lazy again, I swear. Hell, I didn't even go up to the lookout till yesterday, and then.

The shock of it.

For the thing which I greatly feared is come upon me, and that which I was afraid of is come unto me.

I clench and unclench my fists, then remind myself that it could have been worse. The figure I saw through the field glasses was a tiny speck, far in the distance. He could have been closer, could have been HERE.

But no. A let-off. By the grace of God.

I take a breather before the final slope, then launch myself up the face of the hillside in the old way, thighs pumping, hands grasping branches and propelling my body past them, on to the next, to the last. At the top, I bend double and vomit up my meagre breakfast. Afterwards, light-headed but relieved, I walk through the plateau of redwoods and savour again the great ecstasy I first knew when I discovered this place. Eight years ago now, another lifetime.

I reach the Knowing Tree and look up its length, the upper branches vanished in mist. As I climb the first ladder, I think of my children. Worry about them. Fear for them. But they are safe and warm in the ark: the door is locked, and Alice has the key, if anything were to happen. Which it won't. And they have Goldie to protect them. He would lay down his life for us, that dog.

As I climb the second and third ladders, I think about nothing but the knifelike pain in my chest. At the top of each, I rest until my breathing's back to normal. I don't look down. I climb the last ladder, entering and exiting the cloud of vapour, and finally collapse onto the platform.

When my heart's slowed, I stand up and walk to the edge. I grip the low wood railing and look out, down, across: three hundred feet above the ground but all I can see is the mist, with treetops emerging from its whiteness, thousands of them, naked and evergreen, circling this bird's nest. And then, beyond them, the sea. Stretching out in all directions till it meets the horizon. The silent, waveless, colour-changing sea that has guarded this island since the flood.

I pick up the field glasses and touch them to my eyes. A dazzling blur; I twitch the focus. And there, *there*, closer than yesterday, the dark mark that tolls the Bell of Dread inside me. He is coming, still.

I take the paper out of my pocket and unfold it, glance through it again. Yes, I think it gets the message across. But will it reach him? Will he read it? I must write a dozen, a hundred letters like this one and send them out in bottles across the quiet ocean. Surely one of them will find its way to him, will scare him away, stop him encroaching on our paradise and staining it forever with the filthy stench and lies of Babylon, whence he cometh.

Him. The stranger. Whoever HE is.

II

Soon as I breath in I no. The airs not cold on my I-lids like befor its warm an sweet the first blossoms mixt up with pine an grass an stonesmells all sharp from the night-fallen rain. I no shure as I no my names Finn an Ive got a hunerd an four moons. Shure as I no I live on an I-land an my Ma died wen I wer lil. Shure as the suns the sun an the seas the sea I no winters finely over. I stretch my arms an legs genst the sheets an let all the air out my lungs in a long low sigh. Springs here I hurray in my head. Then I breath in a gen.

I sit up an open my eyes an I can see the rainbowish light coming thru the gap in the doorway. The berfly in my chest shivers its wings. Quite as I can I crawl out from under the blankets an climb down the bunk ladder. Alices wheezing slowly so I no shes still a sleep but Daisy must be up all ready I can see her bed in the dim gold sunstreak an the pillows empty. Theres jus a hollow dint where her heads been.

I find her in the kitchen drinking milk her top lip painted wite an her fingers an thumbs cageing the cup tight like its a bird or a rabbit strulling to scape. Morning Daisy I say an she looks up all bleary from the cup an smiles. I ask her where Pa is an she shrugs Out like its a question cus she dont realy no the anser. Erly mornings shes too deep in her milk an dreams to pay any tension to wats round her.

I drink some milk its still warm an it makes me feel bigger an easier some how. There are pancakes on a plate in mill of the table but theyre cold so Pa musta made em befor he milkt the goats. I wonder where he is now. Some days hes gon all morning but its rare. I fetch some chopt wood from the pile an fill up the range. Alice reckons he goes up to the Afterwoods but she dont no shes only magining. I eat a pancake with blackbree jam an finish the milk an wash the cup then like all ways I por milk in a bowl an put it on the floor an yowl sheeck chush-chush but like some times Snowy dont come. He must be out hunting lizards I magine or licking him self some where in the sun.

I put on trainers an walk outside. The sun feels so good on my skin I want to open up like a flower. I look at Pas mometer on the south wall the mercrys up to fourteen all ready an the rometers arrows pointing to sun. I no its go-ing to be a beauty full day.

I side to serch for Pa cus I want to ask him bout God. I jus gun reading the Bible an its strange an scary like be-ing lost outside at night. Its like the words dont have the same meanings they had in the Tales. An all them people be-ing born an kild an harly no thing in tween. An God. I cant stand God.

I look round near the chicken shed for Pa but he int there an the doors still bolted. I open it an out they flurry shrawking leven brown hens an the two cocks like kings in ther shiny blackanwite robes an rubberish red crowns. I throw em some corn an watch. The hens peck each other moren the food shrawking an grobbling ther beady eyes all ways open. Pa says theyre jus like people in the befor world eaten up with envy for all the things they hant got an not membring wat they do. But they lay eggs an ther flesh tastes good cookt so thats wy we keep em.

I go in the shed an pick seven eggs from round a nother hen whos I-ther laying or sitting. There are maybe mor under her but she pecks my rist wen I try to lift her up. I hold out the edge of my T-shirt so the eggs lie hard in the soft hollow clicking like stones in a pocket.

I take em to the kitchen an place em in the straw box. Daisys reading now she looks up an asks me wat an ogre is. I splain bout em being giant an eating people an her eyes widen. Its jus stories tho I shure her an she says Ohh an gins reading a gen. I miss the Tales I loved ther once-ponatimes an ther dangerous ventures an ther happy everafters. I liked magining my self a Prince fighting ogres an witches but the Bibles not like that I cant magine my self Cain or Noah or Abram an no body fighting God ever wins.

So out I go a gen round past the chickens an the bamboo hut an the yard of vines an up to the gardens. I guest Pa might be there but he int. So I walk past the rows of tatoes an pumkins an thru the new plowd fields where the cornll grow in summer till I come to the orchard.

I go up to the big cherry tree an climb its branches high as I can. From up here I can see all the gardens an the toy-seeming ark an the antlike chickens an the slope down to the beach an the shining sea. Theres no sign of Pa so I turn round an look up past the goats an sheep an the river an the lake up to where the trees grow taller an closer to gether till my eyes cant make out the spaces in tween em cus theyre all dark with shadow an the treetops rise ever higher on the hill steepning behind. The Afterwoods. Towring over us like all ways. My mind goes kinda blank an I look up at the sky. Its blue sept for one wite line like Gods scratcht it with his nail.

I feel thirsty so I jump down from the tree an walk to the river. I neel down an drink the clear I-see water. Its so good an cold I plunge my hole head in an after I rub the hairs dry. I breath in deep an I can smell the dark mud of the rivers bank. Then I close my eyes so the blood in my lids is luminated an all I sees red an I listen. I all ways hear sharper wen my eyes are closed. I hear the bird that sounds like its singing in questions an the bird that sounds like its sucking wet sand thru its beak an the bird that kinda shrawks like its angry. I dont no the names of the birds Pa says he never lernd em. An under all these sounds I can hear the river shushing thru its bends. An me. All ways me. I can hear the air go-ing in an out my mouth an wen I hold my breth I can hear my blood booming quitely like the thickest string on Pas guitar. Duum duum it goes. I wish Ikerd stop it some times so Ikerd hear all the other sounds clearer but Pa says without that duum duum I wunt hear no thing a tall.

I can feel my belly rumbling an stirring now so I go to the dark bend where the spade is an dig a hole an crouch over it the flies zizzing near my face an cool water rivering down my temples. In winter you cant smell wat you do but todays heat minds me of summer an the bleurch of it under me. I wipe my ass with dock leaves then throw em in the river where theyre carried a way. Then I cover wat I done with erth an wash my hands.

On I go feeling lighter. Its hot in the sun so I walk long the side of the lake an up the slope till I reach the smaller trees at the edge of the Afterwoods. Now I turn left an walk thru scatterd shade edging the forest an looking side ways into its climbing darks. I stop an stare an feel sunly spookt. I never been in there a lone. I never been in there all the way. Pa says the heart of its dangerous. Cording to Alice theres a tree deep in there calld the No-ing Tree. Alice says Pa told her bout it once how it tells you secrets of the I-land an he promist wen she had a hunerd an sixty moons hed take her to this tree an shed no all. Shes got a hunerd an fifty nine now an Alice says if he dont take her nex moonday sheal go a lone. She dont say that to Pa tho only me an I dont be leave her. Her mouths biggern her belly Alice.

I keep on walking the forests edge my trainers shushing thru long wet grass. Ahm looking for Pa an for Snowy. I pass some traps but theyre emty ther steel mouths open waiting.

On an on I go the airs dead still an I start to grow fear full. I gin calling ther names.

Pa.

Snowy.

Pa.

Snowy.

Finely I spy him on the rising an run tords him calling. Pa. Pa. Pa. I cant stop my mouth making a smile it wer so creepy an lone some in the shadow of the Afterwoods. Hes with Goldy who waf-wafs me. I run fast as I can tripping over treeroots an brambles. Pas stood still his face shaded his arms held wide an he bends low as I rush an stumble into him. I can smell him like all ways its shuring his smell an his arms go tight strong warm round my back an lift me up an I feel safe in love my eyes are closed.

Wats up sofs Pa. His voice sounds strange.

I dint no where you wer I blurt an he says

Finn you no I all ways come back dont you. You no ahd never leave you for long.

His voices so strange I have to open my eyes an look at his face. Theres a spression on it I dont call seeing befor kinda like worrying an keeping a secret at the same time. To scover wat it means I make my face like his an straighter way I can feel the poison toad squatting heavy in my chest. Thats weird I think wats Pa got to feel guilty bout.

Wats rong I ask staring in his eyes theyre brown an black an wite with yellowish patches an tiny streaks of red an they flick a way an sunly I no.

Mindreading a gen Finn he mutters like hes tired like its a question he all ready noes the anser to.

Pas staring at the treetops. Some things happend I no it.

He sighs Finn I got some sad news. It flashes inside me wat it is an then the black birds flapping in my chest.

Snowy I breath.

Pa nods Hes dead. I close my eyes. Sorry Finn I dint mean it to happen I left all the traps near the woods but he musta gon too far. His words kinda fade.

My hands in Pas an weare walking to gether cross the slope. Its not far but it feels like weare walking a longtime some how. We go past Alices field which all ways looks emty an rong to me without her sun flowers. Then weare in a shadowy part the grass long an I can see his wite fur like a shock in a prest down hollow. I bend closer an see him curld up like hes a sleep. Snowy. Theres blood on one paw an his mouths open like he got stuck in mill of a yawn but wen I touch his side its warm an the furs soft. I gin to stroke him half specting to hear his purr but theres only the birds an Goldys panting an my own duum duum. Snowys lost his duum duum long with his purr.

My I-balls itch an I rub em till all I sees bright stars an flames. Pa whispers Ahm sorry Finn some where bove me. I had to put him out his misry he says an his big hand gentles the back of my head. My face creases up then an the tears come down so hot an fast its like my eyes are poring blood. An my body shivring like in winter an my mouth making a noise I cant stop like ohnohnohno. Pa hols me tight from behind an says my name. Goldy sniffs an whimpers he noes some things rong.

Weare like this for a wile an then Pa lets me go. He rubs my hair an bends down over Snowy. He loosens the trap an picks up the wite body an passes it to me. Snowys not Snowy any mor. Its jus the body he used to wear. Its heavyern I spected an pletely stiff but I hold on to it the tears coming softer now an landing in the fur making lil grey circles. I can harly breath my nose is so glued with snot.

I want to bury him I say. My voices all crowky.

Pa says come with me I no a good place we can put a stone on the grave an rite his name an grow flowers round the stone if you like.

An we walk down the hill out from the trees into the sun. An I feel it on my skin a gen so warm an good an I wonder how such a sweet morning turnd so bad.

I follow Pa round near the rocks bove the sea. He shows me a path that goes to a lil spinny of trees on ther own. Its a peace full place. The trees shelter yer back an sides an you can look out at the sun flected on the sea an the rising where sky touches water. Its all blue today you can harly see where one gins an the other ends. Pa uses a pick to dig the hole. It dont take long. I put Snowys body inside an Pa mutters some words I dont stand an sprinkles erth over the body. Wen I see the dark ness on his wite fur I start weeping a gen but silent now. An I member difrant times stroking Snowy an how he used to jump up to my shoulders an rub his face genst mine. An I smile an cry to gether like wen you get a rainbow. He wer a lovely cat.

Soon the holes fild in an Pas put a big round stone on top an ritten SNOWY on it with a nother stone. We sit to gether near the stone an slowly the tears stop coming. I breath an sigh an look round in the silents. The trees an sky look difrant some how. Inside I feel lighter less bad than in the weeping but kinda hollow like I never felt befor. The trees an sky look greyer thats wat it is. Mor distant. Like theyre not mine any mor only trees an sky. Like some body took the I out of I-land.

But who cud do that. Not even Pa. An then I member God an how He drove the man an woman out from the garden an how He drownd all most all the creatures on the face of the erth an I no it wer Him who did it.

III

There's still snow in the shadows, but during the half-moon that's passed since I first caught sight of my enemy, the springtime's started coming through. I can see it in the Mountain Daisies and Indian Warriors sparkling like shards of sunlight and drops of blood all over the new-green grass. I can hear it in the clouds of swallows screaming as they swoop crazily over the lower treetops. More than anything, though, I can feel it in the looseness of my muscles as I climb towards the sun. My very bones seem to sigh with relief.

And then I reach the top and look out through the glasses again, and the relief shrivels and petrifies like a snake's head in fire. I stare at the dark mark with my heart clanging like a tocsin. He has not turned around. He has not sailed away.

Did any of the bottles reach him? Surely the message within would have. But no, I should have known it would make no difference. He looks so tiny, so vulnerable from here. If only he were the ant he now resembles and I could crush him beneath the tip of my thumb, printing gore on the bluegreen flatness beneath, or push him down down down into the water to drown and vanish like every other creeping thing that once crept upon the earth. Why did this one have to survive, O Lord? Why do you send me such trials when I.

They must not know.

I lift the glasses and look farther west. Past the horizon, below the waveless sea . . . somewhere over there must be the City of Angels, where I lived all those years. Where I sat in a robocooled office, staring at a monitor or doodling on a Rite-Me or cradling my head in my hands and waiting for the pain behind my eyes to go away. The feel of the smooth tight clean-smelling cotton on my skin; the pressure of the tie knotted at my clean-shaven throat; coffee and cigarette smoke in my mouth: almost tastable, the memory . . . but a lifetime ago, a world away. Thank God. For without are dogs and sorcerers and murderers and lawyers and copywriters and WHOSO-EVER LOVETH AND MAKETH A LIE.

Calm down, calm. You know what happens when you get like this. I press one palm against my sweatshirted torso and feel the bone, flesh, fluttering muscle beneath. Don't disturb the wasps' nest. I take deep breaths.

All gone. In the past. Lost forever.

I move to the eastern side of the platform and look out. A vast stretch of nothing glares back at me: pale sky melting into pale sea. But somewhere out there, I know, is (or was) the City of Devils – New Orleans – where I was born and went to high school, where my parents were living when . . .

I close my eyes.

The great wave that crashed down on us must also have drowned them. I know it with my head but feeling it in my heart is something else. Too hard.

Ma and Pa. Strange how the words can have two registers. One (doomful and reverberant) for the sound inside me when I think of them, and another (softer, sweeter, simpler) when Finn or Daisy say it to me.

Pa.

I love you Pa.

I remember when I was five years old, it must be one of my earliest memories and I don't know how much is real and how much I've imagined through the years of guilt and shame, but if I close my eyes now I can kinda see it, swimming, fading, coming back into focus like the sea through binoculars: our house in Davenport Street, the day we returned from the motel. The day after the flood subsided. My first flood, way back in 2005. I remember the empty roads, the eerie silence. I remember the triangular stain of sunlight on the front of our house, the roof unsmashed, then turning round and seeing Mrs Darley's place with a big old oak tree growing upside down from its roof, the ripped-up roots reaching blindly at the air. And the sidewalks smeared with filth. And the stench of blocked drains, spilled trash, dead bodies. And the quiver in my belly when I saw that pack of dogs killing a cat: dogs that used to be pets, their jaws now slick with drool and hunger, eyes wild. And I remember (though I wish I couldn't) pushing past my younger brother Eddie as we entered the driveway so I could reach the other side, the safe side, away from the dogs. And I remember (*please forget*) my father barking DON'T BE A COWARD SON, the white contempt in his eyes, and my shame. And that was only a small flood. What must the cities have been like in those final moments of the Big One, panic rising up with the water level, humans turned to rats on the Day of Judgement? O even my upstanding, courageous Father might have been frightened then. Even he.

I open my eyes and look out again, but there's nothing visible except for blank sky and reflecting sea, the horizon circling . . . and the dark mark.

They must never know.

I climb down the ladders and walk out through the Afterwoods. At the forest's edge I turn left and walk along the shadow line, mechanically checking each of the traps and taking some small vague solace in the beauty of the morning mist over lake and sea. The stillness. The silence. At a moment like this you truly could believe we were all alone in the world.

And then the God-damned cat comes out of nowhere and yows so loud it makes my heart start rattling and buzzing like before.

I've never liked cats.

'Hungry?' I ask, looking it in the eyes. 'Yow,' it replies. 'Yeah? Well, so am I. Fucking get used to it.' It yows again and I kick it out of the way. It stares at me outraged, as if it cannot believe I would dare do such a thing. I hiss, and it retreats a little. Then I begin walking again and it YOWs and YOWs, sliding in front of my boots, scrabbling up my calves, staring at me as though I were evil GUILTY evil and it wanted to tell the whole world my secret crimes. I can see the damn red stains at the edges of my vision now, and I kick it aside again, harder this time, but it makes no difference, the scrawny white fucker comes back again, again, again, YOWing and YOWing, failing to take the hint, and finally the cat the trees the grass the sky everything in my vision turns deep scarlet and I pick the blood-coloured beast up by its tail and it scratches my arm and I yell in pain and fury and fling the fucker. It hits a tree trunk and falls to the ground with a small *crump*.

I close my eyes.

When I open them again, the sky is blue, the grass green, the trees brown, the cat white. The cat doesn't move. I walk up to it, feeling sick, and touch its throat. It's dead. 'Fuck,' I whisper. The cat belongs to Finn. How will I tell him? He'll be so.

And then I get an idea. I pick up the dead cat and put it in one of the empty traps, letting the steel jaw snap down hard on its hind leg. With a little luck, Finn will discover it by chance and figure the story out for himself.

Satisfied, I begin walking back to the ark.

IV

I spy her hidden round a boulder jus her bare calf an its shadow poking out. Her calfs wite genst the yellow of the sand an the greyblack of the shadow an its sloping down cus her nees up an bent. Now I look I can see her footsteps in the sand go-ing up to the boulder. I walk softly cross to her. Wen I get closer I stop an listen. All I can hears her breathing an a kind of fast whisperd scraping.

I step out from behind the boulder an say her name. Alice looks up like shes not realy sprized an mutters Come to spy on me Finn. Her eyes which are black an silvrish blue an wite an longlasht look up at me thru the like dark water fall of her hair.

No Ive come to get you.

Wy.

Snowys dead.

I dont no wy but I can feel my mouth wanting to smile wen I tell her like its funny or ahm barrast or some thing. Its strange cus I no how sad I am truely. I look a way an cover my mouth so Alice dont see. Her voice comes out softer wen she says

Oh Finn. How.

Caught in a trap. We buried him. He wer still warm.

Theres silents an then she says Finn ahm sorry you loved that cat dint you an she hols her arms open like some times at night wen she wants me to cull her. I swallow an stand still. It feels rong in daylight some how. She looks at me for a bit an then mutters some thing an looks back down. Thats wen I mark wat shes got in her hands a sheet of paper an a ninkpen. My brows make a V an I say

Theyre Pas arent they.

Alice dont speak a word but gins to rite. I see black up side down lines on the top part an finely stand that this wer the scraping sound I herd befor.

Wat are you riting.

A letter.

Looks like moren one.

She stops an looks up with a crinkly smile that I no means shes mocking me. Theres some thing I hant stood. Wat I snarl.

Not a letter of the alfa bet Finn. A letter like a message.

A message I echo.

You member that bit in the Tales where theres a man on an I-land Alice asks.

Soon as she says it the pictures in my head of an I-land I never realy seen a bit like ours but difrant cus that wer how it wer scribed in the Tales. An a man with long hair an a beard like Pa. An trees calld palm trees which I magined with hands for leaves but Pa said they werent truely like that.

In that story the man rites a message an puts it in a boll you member Alice says. An he throws the boll out in the sea an it floats a way. An then one day some body in a nother land scovers the boll an reads the message an comes to rescue the man from the I-land.

Yeh I say tho in truth ahd forgot all that part with the boll.

Well thats wat ahm do-ing says Alice like thats the end of it.

I dont no wat she means so I jus say Wy.

I jus want to no if theres any body out there she shrugs.

We both look out to sea. The views the same as all ways sept now theres a pack of grey clouds on the rising an the bird with the angry shrawk is gliding round an round in the high blue.

But you no there int I sist.

No I dont. How do I no.

Cus Pa said.

Thats not true. He said he dint no. He said it wer impossle to be shure.

I frown trying to member but its like looking at some thing thru mist or rain I cant realy make it out.

Its like we dont no if theres life on any other planets says Alice. There might be or there might not be but we dont no.

I think bout this for a wile an then I ask

So wat does it say.

Wat.

Yer letter.

Not telling.

Dont be stupid I snort an try to grab the paper but Alice hides it behind her. Its private she says in an I-scold voice.

I get a shoot of black anger an hate for Alice then an the tiger in my chests roaring bigteetht but Pas tol me I shunt ever tally-8 so I push the shoot back down a gen an say You coming to eat.

Soon.

Dont touch the water I mind her.

Alice rolls her eyes an mocks Yes Pa.

The tiger roars a gen but I jus shrug an walk on up the beach breathing too fast an fitting my feet in the holes in the sand I made befor coming down. Wen I get to the marsh grass Ive calmd down a bit. I stop an look round an I see Alice standing by the waters edge an some thing bright that I guess is a boll floating slowly a way from her. I walk up the slope to the pines an wen I turn round nex Alices started following me her eyes on the ground like shes thinking of deeps. Out in the sea the bolls jus a faint dazzle on the rising.

The guitar makes that clungky echo sound wen Pa puts it on his nees an we all go silent. Weare in the fire room like all ways but the fires not lit. Its not cold tonight an I can feel the warm coming from the range in the kitchen. All the lights coming from the candles on the walls an the table. I watch Pas fingers move over the strings smooth as river water over stones.

Like mos times theres a duum duum that Pa calls the rithum. This ones fastish an sounds kinda happy. At first I dont member it so I think it must be new but then the words start an it comes back to me.

Well he got real mad with the sinners an sided he orter
Let rain fall till the hole erth wer covered in water

Theres candlesmell in the room an in my mouth still the taste of pumkin soup. Pa an me workt thru the after noon on a new garden. My back an shoulders ache from digging an my skins brown an buzzing from the sun. Deep inside me tho alls calm an still. It feels good to be tired after working like Pa all ways says.

Noah made the ark like God told him out of gofer wood
An that wer how he an his family survived the great flood

Its the song bout Noahs ark. Course I no that now cus I red the Bible but wen I wer Daisys age I all ways be leaved it wer bout us an how we rived at the I-land. I member wen Pa sung it befor I thought his name must be No-er. Alice an me we scust it after. I said Hes calld No-er cus he noes evry thing an Alice laft an said No hes calld No-er cus he all ways says No. Thats not true bout Pa all ways saying No tho. Truth is he jus wants to tect us.

There wer kangroos an larmas an elfants all in the boat
It stank to high heaven but at least they wer able to float

Wen the songs over Pa takes a swig of wine an says Alice. She picks up her fiddle an bow. Daisy goes cross to Pa an sits on his emty nees an he puts his arms round her an his hairy chin in her neck. She giggles an Pa shushes her. Alice standing up near me hols the bow ready like shes bout to stab a fish an then

Eee-wwerrr.

Wat she plays I never herd befor its dark an slow. I watch Alice for a wile then close my eyes an I see the sun setting over the rising staining the sea like blood an Gods ghost moving over the waters. The songs got no words only string sounds but its beauty full an fear full. I open my eyes a gen an feel a shock cus Alices staring into me like shes angry an the musics gon jagged. But then her eyes kinda float thru an outta me an I stand that she wernt angry wernt looking at me a tall only see-ing the music an now the bows weaving sweet meldy from the fiddles neck jus three or four notes over an over but its power full sad. In the silents after Pa asks her wat it wer an she says

I jus vented it.

Truely says Pa. It wer strornery Alice. You got a title.

Theres silents then Alice says Song for Snowy an she flashes me a tight lil smile. Then its gon an shes putting the fiddle an bow back in ther case.

Nex I do some bird songs I been praxing. Pa shakes his head an says Thats mazing Finn. I smile an look at the floor. Pa can harly whistle a tall him self.

Daisy stands up an sings her favourite the song that goes

Its raining its poring
The neighbors ignoring
They laft at our boat
Till we started to float
An they were all dead in the morning

Then we all join hands in a circle an skip round singing

Rainy rainys falling
The wether is up alling
Splish splash
Glug glug
All gon now

We do it five times faster each time so by the end weare all laffing on the floor then after a wile we calm down an drink some wine an Pa picks up the guitar a gen. Them fer milyer notes come out the echo hole an Alice gets her fiddle out an pares to join in. I love this song it all ways makes me happy an shured. Pa rote it the day we rived at the I-land. I start tapping out a rithum on the wood floor with my feet an Pa an Daisy sing to gether ther voices like the sea an the sky.

Morning has broken like the first morning
The great wave has broken like the first wave
Be cus the rain came an drownd all the sinners
We live on this I-land an we are all saved

The meldy gins slowish an all mos sad but soon like all ways weare speeding up an Alices fiddles whooping an ahm pounding the floor an the walls an weare all dancing even Pa with the guitar hanging from a strap round his neck. An hes singing like its the last song weare ever going to hear.

The old world wer dying but now we are living
The sins of our fathers are all washt a way
Be cus the rain came an kild all the liars
We no only truth now like on the first day

By the time the songs ended weare all kissing an culling an the rooms spinning round us in a smoky blur. I can feel the hurrays shooting thru me.

I lie in bed closing an opening my eyes trying to see the difrance tween the two darks but I cant. Like some times the thought of the dark makes the black bird thats in me flap its wings. I magine Ive been buried under ground an wat I sees the erth packt tight to my I-balls. Or worse I magine the darks a black cape held down over my face by Pa to put me out my misry. *And Abraham stretched forth his hand and took the knife to slay his son.* I sigh an breath an coff jus to hear my self in the room an then I hear an ansring sigh from Alice. She turns over in bed the sheets shushing an I hiss
Alice.

Yeh.

I liked that song you did. For Snowy.

Theres long silents so I say her name a gen.

It wernt realy for Snowy Finn I jus said that cus I dint want Pa to no the truth.

I wernt specting any of that so I jus say Wat. Wy.

The true title is Song for Ma she whispers. But last time I askt Pa bout her he went mad at me you member.

I dont member. I hate it wen Pa an Alice fight tho so some times I blank out ther words or I blank out the memry after.

I been thinking bout Ma a lot says Alice. Her voices quite an still like shes talking to her self. Some times I get pictures of her in my head specially at night. I see her face an her hair that wer like mine you member all dark an long an curly. Her eyes wer blue like mine too. You an Daisy are mor like Pa. I member Ma telling me that once.

Theres a longish pors then an ahm bout to speak wen she sunly starts a gen her voice stronger.

I dont have many pictures of her in my head only five or six but in two of em shes here.

Here I echo.

On the I-land.

I kinda snort an say Well thats rong.

How do you no.

Cus Ma wer never here. She never made it to the I-land. She died saving Daisy dint she.

But in my pictures shes here Alice sists. I member it.

Maybe yer magining it I say. Like in dreams.

I no wats real an wats a dream Finn.

But Ma died in the sea I say louder. She never reacht the I-land.

An Alice says How do you no.

Wat do you mean.

You only no wat Pa told you.

Wat do you mean.

Maybe hes lying she says real quite an I yell No hes not an Daisy makes a noise in her sleep like shes murmring in fear or some thing.

Pa dont lie I hiss. You lie.

All right Finn calm down she says I only said maybe he wer lying I dint mean.

I hiss Liar an turn over in bed so ahm facing the wall. My eyes are justed to the dark now an I can all mos see the lines tween the planks of wood till the tears come an blur evry thing. Alice whispers mor lies but I blank her out an feel the lines in the wood with my fingers so I no theyre still there even if I cant see em.

Theyre still there. I can feel em. Theyre there. Theyre there.

V

When they're asleep I leave the ark and walk through cool blackness to the Afterwoods, following the flickering halo cast by the firestick in my hand. In the forest the dark grows closer and I walk more slowly, careful not to let the flames touch the branches and bushes that crowd in on me. I could cut a wider path, of course, but it suits my purpose for this forest to be forbidding. I reach the clearing, move between solar panels and unlock the door of the wooden cabin.

Inside, the electrics hum and I sit down at the desk. But the neon is too bright, so when the computer screen starts glowing blue I switch off the main lights and the familiar chaos of this room recedes into soft obscurity around me. From the first drawer I take out the journal and a pen, from the second drawer a bottle of whisky. I pour a glass, put some music on, have a drink, and sigh. Sanctuary.

In the journal I write about seeing the dark mark again. I don't write about what happened with the cat. One day Finn might read these words, and he doesn't need to know about that. It would only hurt him. So I just say the cat died, and that I buried him, and Finn cried.

Seeing him like that uncorked a flood of love inside me. My son, my son, so warm and skinny, I watched him suffering, stranded in the darkness of this new world he'd discovered – the world of pain and loss – and remembered him as that younger, happier boy who flowered here in his first years on the island. I remembered him jumping up and down grinning and slickhaired the day the rain came, and helping me pick the first tomatoes, and sitting calmly in the evening with his arm round his baby sister, and asking me impossible questions at bedtime about clouds and gravity and angels.

Finn, if you ever read this, know that I loved you. That I love you even now, wherever I may be.

Easy tears come to my eyes at the thought of him reading these words. I hope he never does, of course, but if anything were to happen to me, at least this journal would help Finn and his sisters make sense of. Well, everything.

I flick idly through the ten years of my life recorded here, people and events spiralling in reverse, the floodwaters pouring back up to the skies, back to the first entry, the first sentence: 'There was an earthquake yesterday.' Facing this, on the inside cover, in thick, tall black letters, are the words I wrote the summer before last, after the first of my heartaches:

IN CASE OF MY DEATH OR DISAPPEARANCE
What you are reading now you should only be reading if I have died or vanished from the island. Leave it a day or so, children, but no longer than that. If I'm not back after two days, then something is wrong. I would never leave you that long.

(Do not read this book if am still here or I will be very very angry.)

Until that day, two years ago, when I went out hunting with Finn, I had always believed myself invulnerable, immortal, here in this Eden. But feeling the wasps swarm inside my chest, feeling my legs buckle, my head blur and tumble, feeling my tongue hang heavy and useless in my mouth as I tried to tell Finn not to worry, that I'd be OK . . . well, after that day, I knew I had to leave them some clue to their past, to the nature of the world beyond this island. Just in case.

The song changes and I listen to the unfamiliar chords, frowning. What is this? It's from some compilation I made, way back, during the first years of our marriage. And then I remember. It was one of Mary's favourites. The plasticky ballad sweetens and swells into its chorus – a tune I always hated – and I have to bite the inside of my cheek to stop the tears pricking in my eyes again. Sentimental fucking fool. Your wife's gone and you'll never see her again, what's the point in.

But, disobeying the diktats of my mind, my fingers creep to the mouse and click on the camera icon. An image of Mary flashes onto the screen, wearing a night-dress, smiling. Her belly is huge beneath the loose-fitting cotton: pregnant with Finn. Alice must have been upstairs asleep, and I must have been . . . where? Behind the cam-era, of course: the recipient of that smile; the object of her love.

I groan, rub my face, drink some more firewater. Why must I rake my own heart like this? 'Goodbye, Mary,' I say, not looking at her, and click to the next image.

Mary with her brother, Christian, in the garden of his mansion. I arrow hate at the screen and click again. A shot of Christian with his family: his oh-so sophisticated wife Charlotte and their two stuck-up kids, Will and Chloë. Once upon a time, I had loved those children – my nephew and my niece. And they had loved me. Regret, longing. But then I remember the day of my humiliation, that boiling August, working on their fucking swimming

31

pool, and I click and click and click until the Highfield family have vanished and a new face appears.

It is my face. Or was. Another me. Much earlier, this one, back in the New York office, when I was the young hotshot, the rising star. My hair is cut and gelled in the fashion of the time, cheeks cleanshaven, teeth white, eyes unlined and bagless. I look like any other smart, conventional, ambitious 21-year-old, but behind those eyes, I know, there was only emptiness and greed; the desire to forget my sad, slow, shameful childhood and to burn a new future for myself in the wonderful world of money.

I click to the next image and find myself looking back at me again. But a decade has elapsed between the two photographs, and you can (just) tell. This one is taken in Pacific Palisades, and I am no longer merely hungry and ambitious, but successful, self-assured, happy. I am a married man now, a doting father. I wear a pressed white shirt, the top button open, jacket hanging on the back of the chair, Mary's dream kitchen agleam behind me, the walls blotched with colourful rectangles (Alice's pre-school paintings), my hands (soft-skinned, normal-sized) cupped round a steaming espresso, papers on the table, hair only slightly greyed, expression tired but patient, amused, affectionate, a little vain. He looks like a nice guy, this me, doesn't he? This model executive stroke family man, so prosperous and reasonable and normal, his image haunted and surrounded now by the ghostly reflection of my old, bearded, wild-eyed visage. What the hell could have happened to him? That's what they all wondered, all whispered behind my back, as I began changing from him into myself.

But nothing is ever quite as it appears and I remember, I remember, being inside that head, behind those eyes . . . I remember that day in January, my heart full of small anxieties, as it always was, back in Babylon. I was Godless then, I had no faith. I was worrying about MONEY, as I always did, back in Babylon. I was sat at the breakfast table, scribbling ideas for a new campaign concept. Blood buzzing, chest hollow, mouth bitter. First thing I noticed: I couldn't draw a straight line. Puzzled, irritated, vaguely frightened by this. Delirium tremens? Parkinson's? Next, a sort of high-pitched rattling sound. I turned round and saw the plates and cups and glasses on the dresser all shaking and moving. Now I understood what was happening: there'd been a few small tremors the week before, and the TV had been warning us that a bigger quake was coming. I stood up and felt the floor vibrating; held on to the back of the chair. A glass fell from the dresser and smashed, then mugs, a whole stack of plates. Alice screaming, Mary in tears and lo the sun became black and the moon became as blood, and the stars of heaven fell unto the earth, and every mountain and island were moved out of their places, and the president and the senators and the shareholders and copywriters hid themselves in the lobbies of skyscrapers, and said to the skyscrapers, Fall on us and hide us from the face of Him that sitteth on the throne, for the great day of His wrath is come. And when the quake was over and the city was full of holes and smoke, I looked on all the works that my hands had wrought, and behold, all was vanity and lies, and there was no profit under the sun, and I turned myself to behold WISDOM. And, for the first time in my life, I bought a Bible – that same book which

Finn is now reading, which Alice read before him, and which Daisy in her turn will read next. And I also bought a diary. The diary which is in front of me now.

I look around the dark room, which is still, not shaking, and breathe out, relieved. You were only clearing your throat that day, weren't you Lord? Only warning me of what was to come. But it was enough. Blind as I had been, I saw the Light that day. I sold my cars and began taking the bus to work. I cut up Mary's credit cards and put the villa on the market. As for my 'work', I suddenly saw through it, saw what a sick joke it truly was. After the quake, I could no longer fake interest in what particular combination of words would best help sell sugar-pumped breakfast cereals to borderline obese 6- to 10-year-olds in the fucking Midwest and it was only a matter of time before there were mutterings in corridors, special meetings to which I wasn't invited, a sabbatical to help me 'recharge my batteries', and then, soon enough, nothing at all. No office, no job, no obscene salary or mortgage, only a rented apartment in Crenshaw, a weekly wage for digging swimming-pools, and a sense of freedom, of rightness, I'd never known before. Lord I thank You that I am saved, while they, they are all damned.

Without even thinking, I click on the mouse again, and a picture of Alice fills the screen. Alice in the Pallisades, before the quake. Alice wearing her Silvergirl T-shirt, dimples in her cheeks, ribbons in her hair, a gap where her two front teeth had fallen out. Behind her the sky is blue and the infinity pool glimmers and glints, making a false horizon where it ends and the sky begins. Three years old she was then, a picture of perfect unknowing . . .

O my children. O my innocents. Yea, better are they than all the other people of the earth, who hath not yet seen the evil that is done under the sun. How can I ever tell them? About the world, I mean. About the EVIL. An invisible wave rises over me and the room's dark air seems to press down like seawater as I think of the Stranger – the dark mark – contaminating our island with traces of Babylon, poisoning the minds of my babes. I see their beautiful faces changing, hardening, scowling, smirking, hating me as they breathe the foul sulphur of his words.

They must never ever

I switch off the computer and relight the firestick, then leave the wooden cabin, closing the door behind me. I walk back through the forest paths, back past the lake and through the gardens, back to the ark, where my children are still sleeping. In my bedroom I get undressed and slip under the covers. And I think about Finn again, the shock on his face when he saw the dead cat.

I took him to the cove at the southern end of the island, inside the spinny of oaks, and we buried the beast there. I promised him we'd plant flowers by the gravestone. He turned, nodded slightly, almost smiled. Brave boy. Thou hast put gladness in my heart, son. 'Snowy's body is under the ground, but his soul's gone up to heaven,' I said, and he seemed to grow calmer. He didn't suspect.

He DOESN'T suspect.

Of my killing his cat, of the dark mark out at sea, he knows nothing. *He must never know.* I must never let him see it in my eyes. I must forget it all myself, erase it from my consciousness, drown it beneath the vast and waveless sea.

Holding hands, the two of us stared out at the horizon. You couldn't see the dark mark from there, of course. That was some consolation. Often, I find, it is better to forget what you KNOW, and to believe only what you can SEE with your own two eyes.

The sky, the sea, the empty horizon. The dead cat caught in a trap.

VI

Evry things so green today even the air. I drop the spade to rest my arms an look up at the Afterwoods all mense an shining. Wen did the leaves grow I wonder. I all ways thought ahd mark it the day wen it happend but its like they sneakt out wile I wer looking a way or thinking bout some thing else. Winters no thing but a memry now.

I wipe the swet off my face an pick up the spade. Daisys off below me milking the goats. Alices probly down by the sea thinking her deeps an waiting for her stupid boll to float back. Pas gon to the Afterwoods I-ther hunting or clecting firewood I dont no which. Todays our moonday an theres a weird buzz in the air I felt it soon as I woke. My hunerd an fith Daisys seventy seventh an Pas I dont no how many. Moren five hunerd. But mor portantly or so she thinks its Alices hunerd an sixtyth. Todays the day Pa wer sposed to take her to the No-ing Tree. She askt him bout it at breakfast but he harly spoke a word I cunt tell if he wer angry or spointed or sad.

The spade makes a stoneshattring sound as it hits the erth an my rists hurt. Where ahm digging will be ground for tatoes but wen I look at the dark hole I cant help thinking bout Snowy. Its leven days since he died I counted em an I thought bout him evry one of em. The pains not so sharp now I dont cry. Its mor like the emty ache you get after a bruise only this bruises where my heart orter be.

Leven days. I try to think bout wats happend in the time thats past but its all fused. Like trying to see the pictures on the wall of the fire room wen the last songs playing an the walls are spinning an the airs greyblack with candlesmoke. You cant do it in other words your lost in a wirl. All you can sees lil bits an pieces.

I member see-ing the chicks wen they wer jus born an I member splashing in the lake with Daisy an Pa. I member a couple rainy days an a couple cloudy ones. All the rest musta been like this I reckon warm an blueskied. I look up now tween digs. Far out over the sea theres a big wite cloud. Other wys theres no thing but blue. The same blue as Alices eyes.

Memrys of the talk tween her an Pa come to me as I dig. I try to blank em a way but I cant stop see-ing Pas face wen Alice askt him bout the No-ing Tree. Wat wer his spression zactly. His eyes wer like looking down into no where his brows a V an the lines round his mouth all tight an deep. I make the same spression with my face an try to feel wat comes. The big black bird slowly flaps its wings.

I drop the spade an pick up the fork an think only bout smashing the clods into smooth dark grains. I push down an twist out an lift up. A gen. A gen. By the time the hole beds dug theres swet poring off my face an neck an my shadows come out the other side of me. I look up an see that big wite clouds moved closer over the I-land. Soon itll cover the sun. I stare at it all perly soft an mense an magine its Snowy gon to heaven. Snowy the God.

Then I sigh. Hungers tugging at my belly. I stab the fork in the erth an gin walking back to the ark.

Pas outside skinning a rabbit wen I rive. His spressions cheer full he says he caught two so we can eat stew tonight. I smile at him. Evry things back to normal I shure my self. I go in the kitchen an chop up carrots an tatoes. Theyll warm all day in the pan on the range till theyre like melting wen we eat em tonight. I love rabbit stew.

Daisy comes in with the box full of eggs. Pa says we can have these now she ports so I drop em one by one care full in the pan of boiling water. Ther skincolourd shells float an bob in the silvrish bubbles go-ing tungk-tungk genst the metal.

Pa made weat bread last night. I cut it in slices an put em on plates an Daisy spreds em with goat cheese. Theres lettuce in a bowl all ready washt an ript. Pa comes in humming Morning Has Broken under his breth. He chops up the rabbits an drops the pieces in the hot wine an grease an water mixt up in the pan. Nex he washes his hands then drops in the carrots an tatoes I chopt an some herbs from the garden then he adds a lil salt an hales the sweetsmelling steam. Thats so good he grins an we laf me an Daisy. Weare so leaved.

We all get some wine like all ways on moonday an we go out an sit under the branch roof nex to the ark. Its cooler there. Daisy talks bout the Tale she red last night an I sorta drift in a half sleep letting her voice wash over me. Some thing bout a brother an sister who find a house made of bread an gin eating it then a witch tries to eat the brother an sister. Ikerd member the ginning of the tale but not the end. Pa murmurs some times an asks questions but mosly its jus Daisy. I savour the ache in my muscles an think bout no thing.

Finely Alice rives an we all look up at her specting a grin or thankyou wen she sees the bread an cheese an eggs an lettuce an wine an smells the rabbit stew on the range. Sted she jus sits down in silents. The silents are louder than the talking wer befor.

Pas I-brows go up. Any thing the matter Alice he asks in a calm voice.

Silents. Staring.

Well a toast then. Pa lifts his glass an we do the same. Happy moonday Daisy happy moonday Finn happy moonday Alice.

Happy moonday Pa we say me an Daisy but Alice says no thing her glass int lifted.

Happy moonday Alice peats Pa.

Is it.

Well evry body else thinks so. Wats the matter.

You no wat.

Alice he sighs an I see his face go sad an old. Cant we jus forget that for now an joy this meal to gether. We can talk bout it after.

Have you changed yer mind.

No I hant changed my mind but maybe if I splain mor youll stand wy.

If yer ansers the same then theres no thing to talk bout.

Theres mor heavy silents an the air goes sunly grey. I look up. The suns been covered by Snowy the God. Pa sighs an I look in his face. Hes kinda wincing like he does wen hes got one of his heart aches. Alices hurting him. Scuse me he coffs an gets up an walks a way. Tears are welling behind my eyes. I kick Alice under the table cus ahm angry an I want her to stop.

Ow she says an stares at me. The look in her eyes is I-see.

Spite my trying to stop em the tears leak out my eyes. I turn a way an wipe em off my cheeks. Stop it I say not looking at her. Jus be normal. Please.

Silents. My eyes are closed but I feel her hand soft on my shoulder. All right Finn. Her voices gon soft too. All right. I open my eyes an look at her specting to see morse on her face but theres no thing like that only a spression I no too well eyes narrowd looking a way lips tight an slightly curving. Its cunning. Alice hant truely gon back to normal shes jus tending to for some secret reason of her own. I side to keep my eye on her after that.

Pa comes back holding four strawbrees an Daisy hurrays. Happy moonday he peats handing each of us a strawbree. This time Alice smiles an says Happy moonday Pa like the strawbree changed her mind. The liar. Pa sighs in a difrant way an we raise our glasses an drink. The wines sower like all ways but I kinda like the way it turns my throat warm now an the sleepy waves that swell in my body after a couple swallows. Happy moonday to us we sing an then we gin eating.

Wen weare all full an the foods speard down our throats Alice clears the plates a way. I look at Pas face he dont spect a thing. Its his fourth glass of wine an his eyes have got that bliss full gon look Goldy gets wen you stroke his belly.

We drink some mint tea then Pa says hes go-ing for a lie down.

Can I come asks Daisy.

Shure hun.

I think I might sleep a wile too yawns Alice.

I squint at her spiciously but she only stretches her arms over her head an follows Pa an Daisy into the ark.

At the door she turns round an says Arent you coming Finn. I make up my mind then. Shes up to some thing but she wants me a sleep befor she dares it so I side to fake sleep an then follow her where ever she goes.

The two of us clapse on our bunks in the shutterd dark. Daisys in the other room culling Pa. We both sigh an moan a bit an turn over an punch our pillows an then we lay there like sleepers only ahm lissning hard as I can.

Time slides a way an.

Pssshhh.

My eye flicks open. Her beds emty. I sit up an see her standing near the door her back to me an her fingers on the handle. In silents I lie down a gen an shut my eyes.

Finn.

Whisperd.

Finn.

Louder.

Checking I truely am a sleep. Silents then I hear krouck waaark tlak. I sit up an stare into the dark ness. Shes gon. The doors closed.

Soon as I get outside I see her. Shes walking up thru the corn field her calves vanisht mong the neehigh green shoots. Go-ing fast as a chaste hen an holding a meat nife in one hand. Thru the orchard she goes up an round past the lake till soon I no theres only one place she can be headed. The Afterwoods.

I stand there by the ark an think wat to do. I orter wake Pa now an tell him but hes tough to shake out of sleep wen hes drunk an his tempers like dry leaves it lights up easy. Course if I follow Alice Ikerd land in trouble too but I cant let her go a lone she cud be hurt or lost or she cud find the No-ing Tree an lern some thing portant. Any way ahm curious. Wat kinda secrets can a tree keep.

Soon she spears into the dark of the forest an I run cross the river an long the lakes edge. Finely I reach the shadow line. My eyes take a moment to just to the dark then I see her. Shes wearing a red dress so shes easy to spot. I watch her a couple moments till ahm shure shes following the path. Then I follow her brushing past nells that sting my skin an thorns that scratch it ducking under branches crawling thru bracken thats tallern me. The scents are strong an green here the airs real close. All my skins got like a nother skin of swet.

A way from the path I see some thing big an yellowan-black an shiny half coverd by creepers an nells. Curious I walk tords it. Theres a like normous spade at the front an two glass eyes. Ahm bout to move closer so I can touch the yellow which looks like metal but then I member Alice whos far a head now an I rush back to the path an follow her befor she spears.

A couple times Alice stops an looks round her like shes nervous. I guess its the noises she can hear I hear em too lil pssshhts an crrreeeks an glowm glowms I dont no wat they are. Alice never sees me wen she looks round. I dont need to hide I dont think she truely sees any thing. I try it my self an stand wy. Look round an all you sees trees or not even them jus shapes of darkgreen brightgreen grey-black all kinda moving yet all kinda still. Alices in red but ahm in grey an green. Long as I dont speak or sneeze ahl jus be like a trunk or a shadow to her.

It grows darker an steeper then the ground levels out an I see like a water fall of light up a head. Alice sees it too an stops. Wen she walks into it I follow to the place where she stood befor an I stand wat made her stop. Theres a circle of open ground staind yellowgrey by daylight with four big black squares lying in the dry grass like the windows of a house under ground. But thats not the mos mazing thing cus in mill of the clearing there truely is a house. Its made of wood like the ark but its smaller an the walls go straight down to the ground they dont curve. The windows are square not round. I stand behind a tree an watch Alice as she walks to the door. I think bout Daisys tale of the house in the woods an the witch who wanted to eat the brother an sister an I shiver. Theres some silents then Alice pushes the door an goes in. The door shuts behind her.

I have to wait then Ive got no choice. I sit down by the tree an rest my legs an scratch my neck an arms an wish ahd thought to bring some water. I sit there for ages lissning to the forest an trying to make slyver in my mouth. The time goes so slow I some times magine its stopt all to gether. I think bout the yellowanblack metal thing in the woods an the black windows in the ground an wonder wat they cud be but my minds emty. I grow tireder an tireder so finely I lean genst the trunk an close my eyes.

I open em a gen an get a jolt of fear. The airs cooler an darkern befor an the door of the houses open. I look all round but cant see Alice an wen I look up at the sky bove the clearing I can see the blues gon deeper. It must be evening. I get up my arms an legs numb an buzzing an have to grip the tree cus my head starts spinning.

Venturely I walk cross the clearing. I bend down to touch one of the black windows it feels like its made of glass but I cant see any thing thru it. On I go to the door. Alice I whisper but theres no body. I go in an close the door behind me. Inside the house its truely silent theres non of the lil noises you get out mong the trees. I can hear my self breath. Theres a musty dusty smell like the doors been closed too long. Wen my eyes just to the dark I gin to see my roundings.

An thats wen I gasp.

Cus wat I magined wer only a strange kinda wood on the walls now pears to be some thing I thought dint zist. Books. Hunerds of em by the looks of it maybe even thouzuns. But how. Ikerda sworn Pa told us hed only saved three books from the flood. The three mos portant books of all he said Tales the Bible an Shakespeare. All the other books in the world came from these he said. Maybe ahm membring rong I dont no.

I move near a wall an start reading off titles theyre in alfa betical order. DEFOE Robinson Crusoe. DHAL-GREN Samuel R Delany. UNDERWORLD Don DeLillo. WHITE NOISE Don DeLillo. US ARMY SURVIVAL MANUAL: FM21-76 Department of Defense. I stop reading an look round the rest of the room. Its a mess. Theres junk boxes papers tools all over the floor an in the mills a table you can harly see the wood of for all the things piled on it. Theres like a shiny wite box with a black tanglar face which tapt on it feels like glass. The other side of it looks like stone but its not as cold or heavy an its got like rubber snakes coming out of it. Nex to that theres a flat wite box covered in lil squares an each squares got a letter of the alfa bet or a number or a shape I dont stand on it. Theres all so a blue metal insect with a witish glass eye in its head an papers all over the table covered in lil black letters. Ahm bout to read some wen I hear a noise from outside like a bird shrawking or a.

Or a girl screaming.

My heart beats fast an I run to the door.

Outside the airs bright nex to the air in the house but wen I look up at the sky I can see the blues gon purple-black an all the lights coming from the moon. Nights all ready fallen. I wonder if Pas woken up yet. If he has heal be worried bout us maybe angry. I close my eyes an listen hard but all I hears the trrrpppt trrrpppt of the cadas. I walk cross the other half of the clearing an enter the closepackt trees on the far side. But I cant find a path in the dark there an ahm scared. Then the sound comes a gen from some where up a head.

Help.

Alice I yell.

Some silents then

Finn. Help me. Please.

She cant be too far I can hear evry word. I start to walk.

Where are you.

Here she says. Over to my left now.

Keep yelling Alice.

Finn.

Keep yelling so I no where you are.

Help me.

Ahm coming Alice.

Finn.

Ahm getting closer.

Snake.

Wat.

Finntheresasnake.

Shit I hiss then

Dont move. Ahm nearly with you.

We keep go-ing like this till finely her voice sounds so close I no Ive found her even tho I cant see her.

Alice where are you.

Up here.

I follow the sound an see her shape dimly on a branch jus bove me.

Wat are you.

I told you. Theres a snake down there. Care full. Listen.

I listen an yes I can hear it the tsstsstsstss that Pas warnd us bout. I stare thru the gloom an reckon I can jus make it out. I try to member wat Pa told us bout snakes but ahm too fraid I cant think.

Wat are you go-ing to do Finn.

I dont no I fess. Maybe if I go back an get Pa.

No she cries. Dontleavemeherewith. She swallows. It.

All right I wont. Calm down Alice. Let me think.

I take a few steps back case the snakes sizing me up an close my eyes. I all ways think better with my eyes closed. I stand like that for a wile go-ing duum duum an then finely I get an I-dear. I dont truely no if its a good one but its the only I-dear Ive got. I serch with my hands on the ground for a stone.

Get ready to jump down I say.

But theres a.

I no ahm go-ing to stract it. Soon as I say Go you go okay.

Silents.

Okay I peat.

Okay she says finely but like she dont truely be leave it.

I stare into the bluegrey an try to see where the snake is. Tsstsstsstss. Some thing moves an I throw the stone near it. I wer hoping the snaked go where the stone landed but it seems to see me then its eyes are on me an its making a difrant kind of noise. I take mor steps

47

backward. The snakes moving closer. Shit I hiss my hearts in my throat go-ing DUUM DUUM. I go farther back till I feel a tree behind me an I cant go any farther.

Jump I shout. Its near me now jump an get a way.

Theres no anser only sobbing an tsstsstsstss.

JUMPDOWNYOUGOTTHENIFESTABTHEDAMN-THINGPLEASEALICEPLEASEDOITNOW.

But non of this comes out its only in my head. My mouths open but its too dry I cant speak. The snakes slith-ring closer. I cant move I feel sick the black birds flapping inside. Help I cry then I hear an see some thing move beside me. Rustle an loom. Some thing big. I cant breath. The big thing moves a sun blaze of light flares over the snake an bracken an trees an the hand of the big thing its a man its Pa an I gasp Pa but he dont speak only keeps moving slowly past me tords the snake thats frozen in the fires light.

Pa moves a head of me closer to the snake an I can see hes got a fire stick in his right hand an a nother stick in his left. He leans the fire stick close to the snake which hisses an cowers an then with the left hand he brings the other stick down on the snakes neck. The other sticks got a V at the end an the snakes heads trapt tween the forks. Then Pa brings the fire stick down on its head an

TSSTSSTSSTSS.

The snakes dead.

The airs heavy in the kitchen like wen a storms brewing. Pa spoons the stew in my bowl an I mutter thanks. Ahm so tired I can harly lift my spoon. No body speaks sept Daisy who keeps looking puzzled in our eyes an asking where weve been. Finely Pa shushes her an says Eat.

I spected Pa to be angry with us. Maybe he is but thats sernly not all he is. All the way home he harly said a word. He askt us if we wer hurt an that wer all he never askt wat we wer do-ing in the Afterwoods he never askt us if we went in the house he never told us wed done rong. He cleand our scratches an stings wen we got home but there wer no love in the way he did it he dint look at us an he dint say any thing. I all mos wish wed been pun-isht sted of these heavy silents. I glimpse his face a couple times wile weare eating but each time he must feel my eyes on him cus he jus sighs Eat Finn an bends his head even steeper over the bowl. I only see his spression for a few seconds but each time it looks like it did this morning wen I made my face like his an felt the black bird. It looks like hes fraid of some thing.

Theres no music. Normly on moonday we sing an dance till the suns all mos coming up out the sea but tonight no body even asks bout it. He kisses us all good-night quick an cold an then he goes. The doors shut theres the sound of his door opening an shutting an then theres silents.

I look at Alice whos sat up in bed seeming zorbed by Shakespeare. I look at her long a nuff for her to feel my eyes on her but she nores me so I read the Bible for a wile all the time pushing a way memrys of the boxes in the house an the black windows in the ground an the tsstsstsstss of the snake in the gloom. *And Er was wicked in the sight of the Lord and the Lord slew him.* The words go thru my eyes an into my head but I dont truely stand em. Ahm thinking bout the rubber snakes coming out the boxes an the words UNDERWORLD an WHITE NOISE. I wonder what White Noise sounds like. Like snow maybe sofly landing on the grass. Or like silents so loud theyre all you can hear. I try to magine an Underworld but all I see in my heads the greengrey sea an them dark shapes you can jus make out thru the muddy water.

Ahm still wondring bout all this wen the room goes sunly darker. Alices blown out her candle. I hear her go hhmmhhmm an look at the shape of her head on her pillow in the dark.

Alice I say.

She nores me.

Ahm wondring if she found the No-ing Tree wile I wer in the lil house. Ahm wondring if she scovered the secret.

Alice I peat. Alice.

Wat she mumbles.

I want to talk to her bout wat I saw in the house an ask her if she noes wat the boxes were. I want to ask her wat she ment the other night wen she said Maybe Pas lying. I want to ask her all this but I dont. All that comes out is

You all right.

Ahm tired Finn she plies in a mumble. Go to sleep.

I blow out my candle an stare at the dark all round me. I wonder wat it is Pas fraid of.

VII

I pour another glass, the red blackish, warm, mysterious in candlelight, and a drop spills on the table. Fuck. It stays in a perfect circle for a moment, then grows longer, tear-shaped, and begins to roll, slowly, slowly, towards the edge. Is it the table that's not straight or is it the floor? Or is it the whole God-damned world? That which is crooked cannot be made straight, and that which is coming cannot be stopped. I bend down my head and lick up the winedrop. It tastes of wood and leaves a purplish stain.

Fuck fuck fucking fuck.

I drink more wine, and look round the ghostly kitchen. The shelves, the worktop, the sink, which I KNOW is all so solid, was all made and fitted by these my hands (battered and tanned like two brown leather gloves on the table before me) neverless looks illusory, solid as steam, in the guttering flameglow. Like it might be swept away by the merest breath of wind. How my life feels, now. I stroke the table with my fingertips, taste it again with my tongue, touch it with my teeth. It's real, it's real. O how I wish wood were flesh, and she . . .

Fuck, I'm drunk, I should go to sleep, but my heart taketh not rest in the night. And wine dulls the dread. And fires the yearning. What life to a man that is without wine? For it was made to make men glad.

Ha.

But it drulls the dead. A little. And yires the fearning.

Fuck, what a day. What a fucking day.

The son dishonoureth the father, and the daughter riseth up against him.

They went to the Afterwoods today, Finn and Alice. While I was sleeping. I woke because I needed to piss, then went to look in on them (how I love their faces in sleep) and. Gone. I left Daisy adream in my bed and ran faster than I've run in years. The wine banging in my temples. Heart booming against my ribs. I knew where they'd gone. Alice has been talking of nothing else for days, moons. She even threatened to go once before, when I.

Tell me the secret or I'll find out for myself.

(anger, bottled)

What do you mean by that, Alice?

You know what I mean.

If you're talking about going into the Afterwoods, I must warn you that

It's very dangerous, I know, you've said.

The consequences of such an action would be.

(her vile smirk, I lost the thread of my thought, spoke louder)

You ever do that and your life won't be worth living, young

My life ISN'T worth living!

Don't ever say that.

I just did. What are you going to do about it, *father*?

(the last word hissed sarcastically, red lights blurring my vision, my muscles hardening, and)

You were asking for that.

(her on the floor, sobbing softly, unconsolably, like a baby, the tender welling of remorse in me, but also righteousness, power, the restoration of order to the universe)

I didn't mean to hurt you but. You shouldn't talk to me like that. I'm your father, Alice, I deserve your respect. Chrissakes we're not living in Babylon now, how can you. Look. I'm sorry. But you drove me to it, didn't you? Almost as if you wanted me to. Come on Alice, that's enough. Here, dry your eyes, blow your nose. Show me where it hurts. Alice . . . take your hands off your face and

(I peeled her hands away, expecting regret, humility, littlegirl love, and instead saw her eyes, one rimmed with a livid red handmark, both blazing)

(fear gouged inside my guts)

I HATE you.

Alice . . .

I killed the snake. They weren't hurt, only frightened. All the way there I swear I thought of nothing but their safety. But, coming back, knowing they were fine, my imagination went wild on all they might have discovered. Maybe it's already too late and they KNOW?

But no (drink more wine), no, I don't think so, I'd have seen it in their eyes. But it's coming. That which is coming cannot be stopped. Coming with the inexorable slowness of that winedrop: the dark mark growing bigger, closer, every day. Always there, and coming.

Briefly I wonder if the stranger might not be a stranger after all, but someone I know. Someone who knows me. Could he have been SENT here? Fuck, I knew I should have. But these thoughts get me nowhere, what's done is done.

I drink more wine it drowns the dread numbs the fear.

Knew I should have ended it when I had the.

Drinkmorewine and drinkmore.

But I

I could kill him. Yes I could. I warned him if he came any closer, and. And soon he'll be in range. Nobody would know. Would they? I could actually.

But would IT stop?

Drinkmorewine.

Or would IT change form and keep coming, coming, inevitable as nighttime? IT's not even him, I see that now. IT's Alice. Alice changing, Alice scenting, Alice asking, Alice wanting yearning needing to KNOW.

Much wisdom is much grief, Alice. He that increaseth knowledge increaseth sorrow.

You promised.

I did not promise, I said maybe.

You said on my next moonday you'd take me to the Knowing Tree.

O why did I ever tell her?

We remember it differently, Alice. There's no point.

The point is you promised, and now you're breaking your promise.

Why? She kept asking and asking and asking about her mother, kept questioning over and over. She missed her so much she was older than the others it hurt her more disturbed her. Finally one night I was so tired so sorry for her I gave her what I thought was a crumb of hope. I said You're not old enough to know the whole truth but, and told her about the Tree of Knowledge. A mistake. THE mistake. Fatal I should never have mentioned it. Because that crumb was not a crumb it was a seed, and it's been growing ever since, growing roots and leaves, stronger and longer and now has flowered. For I have sown the wind and I shall reap

We've been over this a thousand times.

the whirlwind

I won't forget about it, you know. I will keep asking until you keep your promise. I need to know.

Why?

I want to know.

What?

I remember her.

Who?

My mother.

I remember her too, Alice. *Wish wood were flesh. I drink more wine it moans the bed*

I remember her too. Mary. The first day I ever saw her, she wearing that white dress, those pearls, her hair deep brown and done up like that actress's whose name I don't, but O the expensive perfection of her (skin eyes scent breasts hips voice smile) like a CELEBRITY. Out of my league, I thought then, and I was right, but money money money answereth all things. When I saw her again, five years and two thousand miles and one point five million dollars later, it was different. I rang Christian first, her brother: I'd just moved to the Palisades and he was the first Highfield I found in the listings. I told him I was an old college friend of Mary's who'd lost touch. He was cagey, suspicious, till I mentioned the company where I worked, my position there, how good business was. And then: Christian's voice changed. I could almost hear him sit up to attention. Next night in the revolving bar atop the Tallis Hotel we got drunk on margaritas, Christian all charm, the two of us talking MONEY that warmth between us that connection. I hated him later, maybe more than I've ever hated any man, but that night we were like longlost friends, and I told him everything. Silence, the O of his lips when I confessed I didn't know Mary, that I'd fallen in love without ever having spoken; silence, and then that vigorous nodding, the dealmaker's smile, and telling me not to worry, he'd take care of everything. And how he did. Mary Highfield, the faded goddess. I, the risen commoner. Touching the untouchable. The first-date kiss on the steps of her house (lowered lashes afterwards), the second-date blowjob in the warm ocean-scented darkness of my garden (the rustling of silk, the saliva-filled mmm, the bobbing obedient brunette head), and the third-date fuck in room 601 at the Tallis (stripping off those hundred-buck panties and watching that perfect expensive PEACH of

I drink more wine, swallow. Fuck. Drink more wine it bones the spread stop groans the head stop

of an ass upturned, face buried in pillows, so trusting so vulnerable carnal the lips stop drip stop between her stop stop STOP.) More bitter than death the woman, whose heart is snares and nets, and her hands as bands, and her lips as metal traps.

But it is not good that the man should be alone. O no, woe to him that is alone. If two lie together, then they have heat, but how can one be warm alone? How? O

fuck I'm fucked.

I finish the glass and stand up, leather gloves gripping the table's edge till the swaying stops. The kitchen's shivering in the blazing candlestreaks. Half-blind and dizzy I hold on to the table and walk slowly over to the sink drink water from the jug splash some on my face, and breathe breathe blink breathe.

I tell myself it's time to go to bed but my heart taketh not rest and I move into the corridor, hesitating outside their room, the candle in my hand. The door's closed and sprayed with warm light. In my mind flashes a sudden vision of the beds empty abandoned my children gone, but I open and walk through, stumble, mumble (fuck), catch myself, and look round in the halo of candlelight and there they are. Silence, only breathing. Behold, I come as a thief. They there are. Each bed filled with preciousness. O my flesh and blood.

Daisy, little Daisy, in the lower bunk, her body laid out, arms by her sides, rigid and motionless (*like a corpse*) her face blank and whiteskinned, eyes closed (*like a corpse*) her I reach down suddenly spooked and hold a fingertip under her nostrils, feel the warm air and swallow. Thank God. THANK GOD. Her breathing's regular, calm, and perhaps there's the faintest of smiles on her lips. I wonder what she's dreaming. When I ask her in the mornings she never remembers, or never tells, or never dreams (*like a corpse*). Daisy Daisy, I've gone crazy. No. Daisy Daisy, sweet and lazy. O Daisy little Daisy her face and body still roundish fleshy huggy as a baby saying Pa I love you I love you Pa I love you. And when the tears come, Say there there Pa say there there. How I love her smile. And her tears, even if they break my heart.

Above her, Finn *the son dishonoureth* Finn his body writhed in the shape of a backwards 2, face pressed against the wooden wall his blankets bunched up round his neck and calves exposed. I lift the blanket, pull it down to cover his feet, and touch something hard with my hand. What is it? I hold the candle close and see THE BIBLE. He must have been reading it before he fell asleep. I place it on the table near the window and Finn groans, speaks, his voice loud but incomprehensible, like he's talking in a foreign language. Speaking in tongues. *Emlliktnodesaelp*. The sound of fear in his throat and a thrashing of limbs, like he's fighting off a creature in the darkness of his dream. The snake he saw in the forest? I stroke his back through the blankets and say 'There there, Finn, it's only dreams.' He calms, mutters something, then smashes his forehead into the pillow. His body goes limp. Where are you, my son? Somewhere I can't find you, somewhere beyond my reach. Somewhere in the darkness where we all go, into which we are all headed. Inevitably. Finn Finn, the world's all sin. Finn Finn, come back in. Truly the light is sweet, and a pleasant thing it is for the eyes to behold the sun. But if a man lives many years, and rejoice in them all, yet let him remember the days of darkness, for they shall be many.

I cross the room. The candle shakes when I move the flame gutters a drop of wax lands on the back of my hand briefly burns goes hard and cool. Fuck, I whisper. For a moment I see her eyes open. But when I get closer I realise it was only a trick of the light. She's lying foetal, fast asleep, blankets tight to the shape of her. I move closer and hold the candle above her face. Hold it tight so it doesn't drip. Hold my breath so she doesn't hear. My beautiful daughter, my firstborn. Alice Alice, her smiling malice. HOW COULD YOU? To be betrayed by someone I have loved so much. Alice Alice, the poisoned chalice. Alice, my daughter, thou has brought me very low, and thou art one of them that trouble me.

You'll kill me one of these days Alice.

Don't be ridiculous. I'm only asking you to

Every time you ask, it's like a knife inside me.

Yeah? Well, each time you don't answer it's the same for me.

You were my little girl, don't you understand?

Oh forget it, you're drunk

Yes, I was drunk. Am drunk. Always drunk. And always, since the day I raised my hand to you (sorry I'm fucking sorry what do you want me to) the same contemptuous pucker in your lips, the same cold knowing gaze whenever you see me. As is the mother, so is her daughter. O you loved me once and looked at me the way Daisy does now. Didn't you? Didn't you? You did, but you don't remember . . .

I remember. I remember you *before*. I remember the night you were conceived (tenderness and tears after months of jealousy, the relief of being loved after all). I remember the first time I touched you (through the skin of your mother's belly, the soft kick and roll, our shared wonder). I remember the first time I saw you (bloodsmeared and loosenecked, how I feared you were dead) and the first time I woke, the next morning, to discover you between us in bed (the almost shock of you not being a dream). I remember your laughter, the smell of your hair, the lovely weight of you sleeping on my shoulder. I remember the bleary five o'clock breakfasts, wheeling you in the buggy down the hillside from our house, the dawn grey, and the blissful silence of your drifting back to sleep as I reached the beach and the waves shone silver. I remember driving home from work and the two of you opening the door to me, arms wide, smiles serene, you and your mother, Alice and Mary, the loves of my Jesus Fuck why is my pain perpetual and my wound incurable which refuseth to be healed?

I am kneeling now and I am crying, the tears falling into darkness and making no sound, as if this room were a bottomless well and I stroke your back your hip through the blanket, warm like your mother's skin when you were smaller than my hands, inside her. How I've loved you Alice, from that first moment. You have no idea how. And now. You moan softly, a sound I recognise with horror. I take my hands away, suddenly fearful that you will wake and turn your cold knowing contemptuous eyes on me, see something evil in a touch of pure love. And then. She moans and moves beneath the blanket, back arching, legs sighing against the sheets, MY DAUGHTER, and I stand up, step backwards, heart throbbing and candle tipping and wax hot cool on my fingers thumb wrist. She groans like the Devil's fired her yearnings and I know she's LOST to me that she's entered a place where I dare not follow. Like Finn, she is disappearing inside the darkness of herself. His fear, her desire. And I, forbidden, a stranger, am left outside, alone.

At the door I hold the candle up high and look once more at my children, sleeping. I would write their father's name in their foreheads if I could, but the time for that is surely gone. The clay is no longer soft. They have forgotten me days without number, and each new day they forget me ever more.

Go to bed, I tell myself. You're drunk. Go to bed and sleep, you

Fuck.

VIII

First I hear a gunshot then I open my eyes. The rooms full
of silvergrey light an my sisters are a sleep. Pa must be
hunting deer in the Afterwoods I think an straighter way
taste the vensun stew in my magination. Ahm hungry.
Theres been no meat since the cockrel we kild nine days a
go. Pa an Alice an Daisy say theyve got no apper tight in
this heat but my belly feels like theres a deep dark hole in
it. Some times it gets so bad I have to dig my nails in my
skin to stract me from the hollow ness inside.

Outside its hot all ready an the skys wite. The erth I
walk ons iron hard the grasses parcht. I let out the chickens an clect ten eggs from the nest. The chicks are all
ready half grown up not cute any mor but scrawny an
hated by the other hens. I boil three eggs an eat em an
the groaning mouth in my belly quitens down for a wile.

Alice an Daisy still hant stirrd so I walk up past the
field of corn whiches up to my neck now an thru the
orchard to the river. I wash an drink an all the rest then
go on round the lake into the shade of the Afterwoods
edge. Ahm thinking I might see Pa come out carrying a
deer. I close my eyes an listen close but I cant hear Goldys
waf-waf over the summer hum an buzz.

Slowly thru the shadows I walk checking the traps an
thinking bout Snowy an God. I miss Snowy worsen ever. I
dont no how many days are past since he died I lost count
but I guess it must be moren a moons worth. An ever since

the last moonday wen Alice an me went in the Afterwoods Ive felt lone some an fused. All these questions growing in my mind an no body to talk to bout em all. Pas gon real silent hes all ways spearing wile Alice jus nores me if I ask her bout that day like shes shamed or some thing. Daisys too young she dont no any thing. I used to tell Snowy all my fears an maginings it helpt even if he never said a word back only yowld an purrd. Theres jus some thing bout saying the words out loud that seems to make the worries smaller an I miss that. So Ive had the I-dear of go-ing to Snowys stone an talking to the buried mains of him. It wont be the same I no but its a peace full place maybe itll help.

Rounding the rocks I look out to sea. It shines all over like its mercry not water an the risings like a thick black line tween the silverwite sky an the silverwite sea. Ive never seen it so wide befor. Its like sted of touching as they normly do the sea an skyve been puld a part an the blacks the emty space you can see in tween em. See-ing it makes the black bird flap inside my chest tho I dont no wy.

I find the path that goes to the spinny an sell down there shaded nex to the stone with SNOWY ritten on it. Theres no flowers I guess Pa never planted em. Or maybe he did an they died cus I never watered em. Any way I sit there for a wile eyes closed membring my cat how he wer his fur an tail an the way hed jus clapse on to me some times. He loved me I no he did it wernt jus cus I fed him like Alice said. I sit there for a wile thinking like this then it curs to me I came here to speak. So Snowy I gin feeling a bit barrast bout talking to a stone but siding to keep on an not think wat any body else might say if they saw me.

So Snowy I say youve been dead for a hole moon now an I realy miss you.

My throat kinda swells an I have to stop talking. I dont want to cry but the tears come any way an then I think maybe I need to let em out. So I peat

Snowy I miss you. I loved you Snowy an now yer gon I feel real lone some an lost an fused.

The tears are raining out my eyes now. My voices gon crowky but I keep on the words come out in a flood I say

I dont no wats go-ing on now Snowy its like evry thing I thought wer true maybe int but I dont no for shure ahm only guessing. Wud Pa lie to us Snowy wat do you think. Hes acting so strange an distant. An that look in his eyes. Wats he scared of. Ive never seen Pa scared befor an him be-ing scared scares me. I keep thinking bout God an how maybe Pas been talking to Him an Hes telling Pa hes gotta sakry fice me or maybe Hes telling him theres a nother flood coming or Hes go-ing to smite us cus weare wicked in His eyes. I dont no an but then I think Gods ment to be good so maybe Hes go-ing to send us an angel or a mirror cull. But then wy wud Pa be fraid I dont stand.

The words run out then an I sigh. I spose I do feel a lil better. The tears have stopped raining too I wipe em off my face with the backs of my hands an look down at the stone. SNOWY it says but no thing else. No yowls or purrs. I touch the stone like stroking but its jus stone. Its kinda warm but it dont feel any thing an it dont spond. Snowys dead. Ahm a lone. I stand up saying Goodbye Snowy an stare at the mercy sky. Its like the face of God up there. Blank an spression less an terrible bright. Wats go-ing to happen I ask my self. But my self dont no. Only God noes. I stare up at the sky an think maybe God needs to cry. His tears need to rain down. If they clean us or if they drown us I dont no but some things gotta happen.

Walking back I spy Pa an Goldy coming out the Afterwoods. Hes not carrying a deer only the gun. Goldy hears me turns an waf-wafs an Pa turns too he dont look sprized.

Hey Finn.

Hes looking at me but its like ahm not wat he truely sees. I dont no how to splain it. Its like where ever hes looking hes all ways see-ing some thing dark an big that no body else can see. He gins to walk an I go long side of him taking two strides to his one.

Did you catch any thing I ask thinking maybe hes all ready skind an gutted it.

Catch any thing he peats like he dont stand.

I point at the gun hanging from his shoulder. You wer hunting werent you.

Oh. No. I wernt hunting.

But I herd a gunshot.

You herd. His brow makes a V. Oh erly this morning.

I nod. It woke me up.

Yeh. I mist. That wer the only one I saw. Sorry Finn.

Ahm hungry Pa.

Theres plenty tatoes.

Can we maybe catch a fish.

You can try he says in a low voice. I dont no how many are left a live after this drowt. He looks over cross the sea wen he says this an that minds me of the rising.

Pa I say wys the rising so dark an thick. Ive never seen it like that befor.

Its jus a lusion he splains.

Wats a lusion.

Its like see-ing some thing that int truely there. Like the skys a lusion its not blue an its not truely there it jus looks like it is.

I look up at the sky.

Its not truely there.

No says Pa. Lifes full of lusions Finn youl lern that as you get older.

His voices grown softer now softer than its been for a longtime. I feel like hes my Pa a gen like theres a nection tween us. I want to keep him talking like this so I say

I dont stand Pa.

But he ruffles his hair then an sighs. Its hard to splain Finn. Youl stand one day.

Is God a lusion I ask.

He smiles then an I see the old him jus a flash of it behind his sad new mask. No body noes he plies. Some people think Hes a lusion an some people think Hes real but no body truely noes.

Wat do you think Pa.

Theres a real long pors. I dont no. Onestly. I want to be leave Hes real but. I jus dont no. Wat bout you Finn.

I hope Hes a lusion I fess.

He looks at me then like for a moment ahm truely wat he sees.

Wy do you say that.

I want to say Cus God made people an then He kills em cus He askt Abraham to sakry fice his own son cus Hes cruel an pricious an too power full to nore. But non of that comes out my mouth. Ahm worried Pa might get angry with me so I only shrug an say

I dont no.

Pa looks a way he dont say any thing. Weare coming tords the ark now an I no our talks all most over so I say wats most on my mind I say

I miss Snowy.

He winces like hes got one of his heart aches an ahm sorry I said it but then he gentles

Is that where you went jus now. To see Snowy.

I nod an look down at the yellow grass.

I never did plant them flowers for him did I. Ahm sorry Finn. We can do it today if you like.

Okay I say.

An we can go fishing too. Lets go to the lake so even if we dont catch any thing at least we can all cool down in the water.

Okay I peat. I smile up at Pa an touch his hand with mine its got hairs on the back of it. He grips my fingers then sunly lifts me up so Ive got my arms round his neck an my feet dangling in air an his arms round my shoulder blades culling me so tight I can harly breath an his beards scratching my neck an his breths sower but I dont care I feel so leaved. Pa still loves me I tell my self. He hant forsaken me afterall. The berfly in my chest flutters like crazy an ahm so sprized I laf. Its the first time Ive felt my berfly since the day Snowy died.

IX

I untangle myself from Daisy's hot arms (she musta crawled in here with me during the night) and dress quickly in the darkness. I kiss her forehead, damp with cooled sweat, then check on the other two. They're sleeping, thank God.

In the kitchen I drink some water, splash some on my face, then tear off a strip of last night's bread, put a chunk in my mouth and the rest in my fleece pocket. Outside it's still darkish, on one of the longest days of the year. It must be real early – even the cock hasn't crowed yet. I unchain Goldie, rub his ears and shush him, then the two of us hurry through the gardens, through the orchard and up past the lake.

I stand at the edge of the Afterwoods and catch my breath. Below me, the lake is drying up, the exposed mud hard as stone. But what troubles me most is the sea: even in this half-light, from this angle, the horizon looks too thick, like a gap's opened up between the water and the sky. I feel like my whole life, everything I've lived and worked for, could soon disappear through that gap. Is disappearing, now. For that which is crooked cannot be made straight and that which is coming cannot be stopped. *Unless*

I move into the deeper darkness of the trees, and follow the path. The way is so familiar that my thoughts loose their moorings, the thick enveloping woods an unseen blur as I imagine how it would feel to commit The Act. Could it really be so easy? A single cartridge, no heavier than a skimming stone, and the gentle pressure of this index finger, and. The taking of a human life. But so distant, and so justified. He has been warned, after all. And he is coming here to take MY life, my children's innocence and my peace of mind. That whoreson of Babylon. And I, or ever he come near, am ready to kill him.

I am beginning to sweat. Under my hair, below my ears, in the hollow beneath my Adam's apple, in the pits of my arms and legs, the crack of my ass. I stop and look around, lost for a second, then see the cabin ahead, a darkness in the heart of the leaves and trunks and branches. My sanctuary and my armoury. On I go: through the undergrowth, into the clearing. Between the solars, unlock the door. I tell the dog to wait, close the door behind me and slide through cool dimness to the back room. Unlock, open, close. Switch on the light and move to the cabinet in the corner. Another key. The sound of my breathing tight in the silent air. I cough, swallow, open the cabinet, take out the shotgun and the cartridge belt, close and lock the cabinet again. I hang the belt over my shoulder. I break, clean, load the gun. Break it again and carry it back the way I came, locking doors behind me. I will not make the same mistake I made before.

They must never

Deeper into the woods we go, my thoughts spiralling inwards now, the dream recurring: the dark mark in my crosshairs, the dead-still barrel, the evenly squeezed trigger, the shiver of release and the POKK in my ears, then the slow blink, the opening of eyes, the dark mark in the telescopic sights, prostrate and lifeless now, the sun rising, birds singing, the fresh wind blowing through my chest and mind, and they all lived happily ever after. Yes, I frown. Yes, I nod. Yes.

I climb the final slope and pause at the top, leaning against the first of the redwoods. As my pulse slows, I stroke the bark and look upwards into the heavens. *Yes.* I walk towards the Tree of Knowledge. Goldie is already asleep in the hollow of its roots. I unbreak the gun, check the safety, and strap it to my shoulder. Climb the ladder, resting at each platform, my vertigo deepening, steepening as the view below diminishes. I don't look down. At the top, crawling with relief over the wooden planking, I unhook the gun, lay it flat on the platform, sit next to it and take the bread from my pocket. I remove the fleece, eat some bread. Then I take the water bottle from its hole and drink several mouthfuls. Above me the sky is pregnant with morning. The stars are fading, my sweat cooling. I finish the bread and drink some more water. I put my hand to my chest, and count. Ninety-six beats per minute. Too fast. I close my eyes, breathe. In. Out. In. Out. In. Out. Slowly, deeply, forgetting all. After a few minutes I take my pulse again. Down to seventy-four. Good. I stand up and put the field glasses to my eyes, scan the grey distance. When I locate him, I exhale through my mouth and watch for a while. The dark mark. Close now, close to our island; a day's journey max. God hath delivered mine enemy into mine hand this day: now therefore let me smite him.

I put down the field glasses and pick up the shotgun. I kneel before the gunhole and blink through the sights, scanning until I find it again. *It*, not him. The dark mark. The curse of Babylon. Through the sights I can see a head, a torso, two arms, two legs, but no face. It, not him. I inhale, exhale, stroke the trigger. But my knees are aching, I'm not comfortable in this position. I put the gun down and fetch my fleece, fold it on the plank and kneel upon it. Better. I pick up the gun and find It again through the sights. My pulse is speeding. I take deep, slow breaths and tell myself to be calm. Coolness is all. Sweat prickles my hairline, my palms and fingertips are damp and slippery. The butt of the gun hurts my shoulder. I put the gun down, wipe my hands and face on my T-shirt, close my eyes and stretch my arms, rub my shoulder where it's bruised. Calm down, calm. I test my pulse again, it's over a hundred now. Fuck. I lie down on my back, close my eyes, breathe in through the nose, out through the mouth, in through the nose, out through the mouth. There's no rush, I remind myself. Take your time. Chill. As soon as you're relaxed, you're going to ready yourself, aim, fire, and all your worries will be over. What is coming will be stopped. What is crooked will be made straight. All will be well in the eyes of the Lord. We will return once more to the Promised Land. I lose myself for a while in these visions of bliss.

When I open my eyes the sky is brighter, the air warmer. Fuck, I must have fallen asleep. GOD DAMN IT ALL TO HELL. I pick up the gun, kneel on the fleece, blink through the sights . . . and now I can't find him. It. Where the fuck has he gone? I scan the bluish haze, panic rising, then lower my sights a little and there he is. *It* is. It's turned sideways now though, and the angle is more awkward. Fuck. If only I'd pulled the trigger before, instead of. But too late now for regrets. Ready, aim, fire. My pulse is up, my breathing's ragged, but it's too late. Ready aim fire. My hands slipslide on the wood and steel, but too late. Readyaimfire. Sweat drips into my open eye and POKK. I am knocked backward and the barrel bangs against the top of the gun hole. The sound of the explosion echoes in my ears. Frantic with excitement, with fear and hope, I put the gun down and pick up the field glasses, touch them to my eyes, refocus, scan. There, there is the dark mark, and.

It stands.

It is still standing.

I fight an urge to vomit, and stare as it moves out of sight. He must have heard the gunshot, perhaps felt the breeze of the bullet's passage. Maybe he's even wounded. It. Whatever. My enemy is not dead and it knows I tried to kill it. He must hate me, want revenge. It is too late. That which I greatly feared is come upon me and.

Fuck O fuck.

Only on the way down the ladder, nausea hollowing my gut and tingling my fingertips, does the SHAME soak through me. I tried to kill a man. A stranger.

I reach the foot of the tree and collapse on the grass, my back to the trunk. My skin is covered in cold sweat. Goldie barks, puts his paws on my shoulders, licks my face. I push him away and shake my head.

What is this that thou hast done?

I should climb back up and take a second shot. I know I should. But I stare up the length of the tree's body and also know I never will. Too late. Nerve's gone. Fucked up.

And the sky is cloudless once again: no rain today, by the looks of it. And if it doesn't rain soon, the crops will die, the lake will vanish, we will all die of thirst, the horizon will grow wider than the sea . . . and the Day of Doom shall be the end of this time. Let the day perish wherein I was born. Let darkness and the shadow of death stain it.

Fuck O fucking hell.

But, to my surprise, after some time sitting here in the grass, wallowing in shame and fear, these emotions fade and I realise that what I feel more than anything is *relief*. I did not truly wish to kill him. Perhaps I did not even try to. No, thinking about it logically, it was impossible. Shooting at a man from three hundred feet above the ground? Impossible, and I knew it. Only a warning shot. Yes, that's all it was. A warning shot. And who knows, maybe this time he will take the hint? Maybe he will turn around and go back to his island, or wherever it is he comes from?

Yes, I frown. Yes, I nod. Yes.

My optimism doesn't last long. By the time I reach the forest's edge I see only Fear and Hate and Vengeance slouching towards the shore, the mark of darkness growing larger, closer, looming till it blocks out the sun. I stare at the ground as I walk, checking the traps. At least there are no more cats to be killed.

As I think this, Goldie barks and I turn to see Finn running behind me. He is smiling. Vainly I try to mirror his look of happiness.

'Hey Finn.'

He looks in my eyes, and automatically I turn my face away from his gaze and begin walking. I don't want him to read my mind this morning. It's too damned dark in there.

'Did you catch anything?' he asks.

I look at him blankly.

He points at my gun. 'You were hunting, weren't you?'

X

Leaning back genst the dry mud bank I stare up at the oak leaves shining green. You can see ther veins dark an the flesh so bright its like the lights coming from inside the leaf. Theyre beauty full. The fishing rod moves tween my fingers an I sit up but the lakes faces smooth as ever sept for the ducks swimming far off an closer the lil splashes made by the frogs as they jump one after a nother into the lake. Daisys standing in shallow water watching the frogs an Goldys on the bank watching me. Pas talking with Alice some where in the trees behind. Hes jus been with me up to Snowys grave an we planted some flowers in the erth. It musta been a breth of wind moving the rod I reckon an lie back a gen. Ahm ginning to think Pas right. The fish must all have died. Pleasenopleasenoplease moans my belly.

The shade ahm ins grey the skys covered by thin wite cloud. Less thats a lusion too it curs to me. Any way the heats strong as ever. I feel like ahm sitting inside the range my meat an bones slowly cooking. Finely I give up I plant the rod in the mud farther down an go wading into the water. Its warm as blood but nex to the baykt air its freshing an soon ahm pletely merged my body lying flat genst the mud floor eyes closed breth held all my skin drest in soft water. I wish Ikerd go swimming like Pa but ahm not a good swimmer. Non of us are realy he never showd us how. Ive askt him plenty times but he all ways had some thing else to do so in the end I guest he dint want to teach us. I dont no wy. Alice says its cus he dint want us to scape the I-land but the seas poisond any way so that cant be it.

My chest goes tight. I lift my head bove the water open my eyes an hale. The airs like fire. I look round Daisys paddling farther long the bank shes playing some game in her magination talking to her self. Sunly I hear Alices voice from some where yond the trees. I cant make out her words but shes angry I can tell. Her voices loud an spite full I hate it wen she yells at Pa like that.

I lie back an float touching the mud neath me with my hands letting the water lap over my ears nearly to my eyes staring up at the sky. There are two shrawking birds like lil black +s gliding in circles. I cant hear em shrawk cus of the water.

I stay like that for a wile then sit up. Looking round I see Daisy splashing water over her self an laffing. Shes gon in deepern befor. I sigh then go under water a gen. I hold my breth long as I can. Wen I come up my heads spinning an I can see stars an all I hears my own duum duum an hee-haw heehaw. I look cross specting to see Daisy but shes speard. I sit up taller an look round. No sign of her. Then my eyes drift farther out an I mark a lil circle of yellowite hair floating on top of the lake.

Inside me the black bird takes a slow flap of its wings. Theres some thing rong I no there is.

Daisy I say but my voice comes out tiny. Then louder

Pa wats Daisy do-ing.

A couple silents an then

DAISY. Pas sunly screaming.

I look round an see him run thru the shallow water then dive an gin swimming that way he has arms crossing

74

one over the other like plow blades. Goldys waf-wafing an jumping like he thinks its a game. I still cant see any thing of Daisy sept her hair. It looks real neat an pretty spred out on the water like a giant goldish lily pad.

She sunly pears her body lifted up by Pas arms. You can see the muscles in em sticking out. Her faces blank. Pas shouting her name an pulling her over to the bank swimming in a difrant way now like hes pushing thru long grass with one arm. Now hes running with her an her bodys shaking slightly. Now shes on the mud bank an her bodys all still like shes fast a sleep. Pas shouting DAISY an pounding her on the back. Alices silent her mouths an O. Goldy shakes his fur dry then sits real quite an watches Pa his eyes are gon all sad.

I stand up an wade thru the water tords em. Times go-ing real slow. In my chest I can feel the big black bird rising flying flapping shrawking. Pleasedontletherbedead I pray. Please God if You zist please dont let my lil sister die. Times slowd so much its all mos stopt. An but then

A sun spurt of water from Daisys mouth. A nother an shes crying her eyes open looking fraid an Pas voices changed hes still saying her name but now hes not yelling tensly hes like sobbing an laffing at the same time. Finely Daisy looks up round at Pa an Alice an me an tinys

Say there there Pa.

There there hun gentles Pa rubbing her back. There there Daisy evry things all right. Evry things go-ing to be fine. There there.

I look up at the hot wite sky an say Thank You.

The skys low an bruised now. Its gon so many difrant colours I cant even name em all theyre like blood stains in water all merging into each other an growing shifting spreding. Ahm standing on a chair in the fire room my head out the open window breathing in the stormsmelling air. Theres witegrey an silvergrey an yellowgrey. Theres bloodgrey an purplegrey an blackgrey an far off over the sea a sun flash of yellow. Pas lit the fire hes in the kitchen now cooking the fish he caught. That wer good news theyre not all dead afterall. It wer a big one too I can smell it cooking. Mor flashes in the sky an then that sound I can never make with my mouth that sounds like Gods coffing or clearing his throat. Alice an Daisy are culled up on the rug to gether Daisy drawing an Alice jus watching the flames. Goldys a sleep at ther feet. Outside the rains started an evry things smelling sharpern befor. Pine an grass an stone. Then the first KKRRAAKK an the arks walls shake.

I close the window an climb down off the chair. Then I go in the kitchen an ask Pa if he needs help but he says Ahm okay Finn thanks you go an warm yer self with yer sisters. Hes smiling his voices gentle an laxt I hant seen him like this for a longtime. I dont no wat happend zactly but its like saving Daisy from the waters kild the big dark thing he wer fraid of. Its like his fears vanisht.

I sit nex to Daisy on the rug an Alice puts an arm round my shoulder. Daisys do-ing a picture of our ark floating in the flood. The wind howls in the chimny an the flames dance.

Pa brings bowls of fish an masht tatoe an we eat with spoons in front of the fire no body says a word. Slowly the hole in my belly spears an I sigh with leaf. When Pas finisht he says Mmmmm closes his eyes an lies back on the rug smiling. We all watch him. Then he sits up.

Listen children Ive got some thing to say. Wat happend todays made me realize some thing.

His voices big an his eyes are grave.

Wat we say.

I want to say that no thing is mor portant to me than you three. That long as your a live an well I shunt plain or worry cus truely no thing else matters. Ahm sorry if some times it seems I dont love you. Daisy. Finn. Alice.

He looks at us one after a nother deep in our eyes.

Cus I DO.

His eyes are glissning my hearts pounding.

Moren any thing.

I feel real happy but kinda barrast.

You no that dont you.

Theres some silents. I want to speak but my throats too sweld. Finely Alice says Yes Pa we no. Then weare all crying an culling an Daisy says like all mos to her self An they all lived haply everafter.

Pa lafs sofly. Yes Daisy. Haply everafter.

Thats a nice moment I dont no how long it lasts but I tell my self ahl all ways member it.

Jus after theres a massive splosion of noise close by an we all freeze then weare laffing. Ahm glad the storms finely come it dont make me think of doom any mor only that the airs be-ing cleard an evry thing clensed. The rains pounding on the roof an the winds roaring but weare all safe here inside to gether. It minds me of some thing tho I dont no wat.

Like some times Daisy asks bout the befor world an Pa tells us a gen bout the dark days befor the pucker lips an his warning dream an how he built the ark in our garden an we scaped the great flood wile all the other people drownd. Ive herd all these stories huners of times some of em wer in the Tales but I still love to listen to em. Then Alice says

But there wer good things too.

She says this quitely an we all look at her.

In the befor world. It wernt all bad.

Wat are you membring Alice asks Pa.

Bright lights an tall tall houses she says slowly like in a dream. An Ma smelling wonder full wearing a long pretty dress an shiny metals an stones on her fingers an round her neck an like colour full paint on her face.

Paint I shrawk.

It lookt good Finn you dont stand. She looks at me then at Pa. I dont have many memrys but wat I members kinda magical.

Pa nods silent an his lips go twisted. Then he says Wat youve gotta stand Alice is that all them things the tall houses an the bright lights an the shiny metals all them things wer dictive. People grew sest with em they came greedy an dicted an thats wat made the bad things happen thats what made the flood.

A longish pors Pa breathing. Hes looking at Alice whos staring at the floor. I cant see her eyes but I wonder if shes bout to cry.

An an I spose cus you lived in that world for a few years that you wer may be. Taminated.

Wats taminated I ask.

Like fected. Like if the snaked bit you the other night youd have got its poison in yer veins. Maybe Alice got a bit of the befor worlds poison in her veins.

Alice looks up her faces red but her eyes are dry. So wy arent you taminated then she mands. Her voice sounds hard but kinda brill like it might break if she keeps talking. You lived there longern me dint you.

I wer oldern you Alice gentles Pa. I wer mune. It wer the young who wer mos septible to the tamination.

I dont stand I say. Wats

But Pa nores me an puts one of his hands on Alices cheek where a tears finely scaped. Its not yer fault Alice. Not a tall.

Ahm fected you said. Her voices like jelly now I think it musta broke all ready. Ahm taminated.

But your safe here. Your fine. Ahm jus splaining wy in yer memrys the befor world looks so pretty an viting. You stand.

This lasts a question an Pa sits staring waiting for Alice to spond. She looks in his eyes then a way then finely nods.

But I love my memrys I dont want em to be taminated.

The memrys are fine Alice theres no thing rong with em. You orter treasure em. Jus dont be leave in em too strongly cus like mos memrys theyre lusions theyre not real. This I-lands mor of a paradise than the befor world ever wer. An if

Silents.

Flamescraklingrainsmackingthunderboomingwindhowling silents.

If wat Pa.

If one day. By some chance. Hes talking real slow an sighing in tween like hes choosing his words out a big box of other words. If some body from that other world wer ever to come here an tell you its jus like it is in yer memrys you dint orter be leave em. Youve gotta no that the person whos telling yous probly taminated.

I feel my brow make a V. But that worlds gon Pa I say. You told us. Its under water. Drownd.

Probly Finn. It probly is. But you never no. Some others mighta survived the flood like we did. There might be

But hes rupted by a nother KKRRAAKK an BOOOM an the room lights up. The walls of the ark shake in the wind an rain beats down genst the windows an it comes to me wat it is that the storm minds me of. I must be membring the journey we took over the raging seas in the time of the great flood. I must be membring how we came to the I-land.

XI

I wake up and remember. Thank God, thank God. This my child was dead, and is alive; she was lost, and is found. O, thank God! In my dream she drowned again: I saw her hair, in a golden circle, floating on the still hazy surface of the lake and tried to swim out to her, but the water was too thick, too heavy, my limbs were weak, and instead of arrowing towards her I seemed to move farther away with each stroke I took. Around me people calmly asked the same question – Mary, Christian, Alice, Finn, all accusing, Why didn't you teach her to swim? – and I shouted at them to help me, to pull my daughter's head from under the water, but they all said, It's too late, she must be dead by now. Their pitiless voices! Howl, howl, howl, howl! O, you are men of stone. Had I your tongues and eyes, I would use them so that heaven's vault should crack. She's gone for ever! I half-woke, and in my dream and in my mind she was dead. It felt so real. I closed my eyes and tried to give the dream a different ending, but it was no good. Each time I pulled her from the water, her eyes were closed, she did not breathe. And then I woke, and remembered.

She lives! If it be so, it is a chance which does redeem all sorrows that ever I have felt.

I get out of bed, stab on some jeans and walk to the kitchen. Daisy is sitting at the table, reading the Tales. She looks up at me and half-smiles, like today is just an ordinary day. 'Pa, can I have some milk?'

'Daisy!' I pick her up, laughing with relief, and throw her into the air. She giggles and shrieks. I wonder if she remembers what happened yesterday, if she understands how close she came to. But I don't want to ask.

I put her back down on the chair. Both of us are laughing. She stops before I do, her eyes suddenly sober, and says again, 'Pa, can I have some milk?'

I pull a face.

She giggles, then groans, 'Paaaa . . .'

'Some milk?'

She nods. 'And eggs?'

'Sure, Daze. Where are your brother and sister?'

'In bed.' She frowns. 'I think.'

'You were the first one up today?'

'Uh-huh.'

'What're you reading?'

'Rapunzel.'

'Oh, the girl with the long hair? How does that one end? I can't remember.'

'They live happily ever after.' She grins, involuntarily.

'They do? Oh well, that's good.'

I kneel next to her and stare at her face for a few moments as she reads, savouring the gratitude I feel.

She feels my eyes on her and looks up. 'Pa! Please can you get some . . .'

'Eggs and milk? All right, honey, I'll be back soon.'

I kiss her, then go outside. The air's cool and white-grey, like the island's floating not in sea, but in the centre of some gigantic cloud. The mizzle's so thick, I can't even see the chicken shed, but the cold droplets feel good on my face. I close my eyes and breathe in the moisture, the shadiness. Summer's cauldron doused, if only for a day.

Remembering last night's storm, I check on the tomato plants and young trees as I pass them. A few broken stems, some scattered fruit, but nothing serious. Winds of euphoria blow inside me. That which is coming cannot be stopped, but I'm not afraid any more. Was it only yesterday I shot at thin air and believed the end was nigh? It feels an age away, that morning. Since Daisy coughed up water and began breathing again, I feel I am living in a new world: a sweet and precious and living world, which no shadow, no matter how vast, can ever truly darken.

I collect the eggs and milk Cloud, then carry everything back to the ark. Alice is up now, sitting next to Daisy at the table. I enter and she smiles at me, for the first time in. How long? Too long.

We eat and drink together, the three of us. When we've finished breakfast, we all go out to work. All except Finn, who's still sleeping. It's so rare, him staying in bed past dawn, that I decide not to wake him.

XII

The risings speard a gen now. Wen you look tween the sea an the sky all you sees the thinnest line you cant even tell wat colour it is. Shured I turn a way from the sea an look past the orchard trees to the gardens. Pas tending the vines Daisys clecting matoes an Alices washing clothes in the river. Ive jus woken up. I breath in an the air feels cool in my nostrils an throat. Evry things misty grey. I feel kinda guilty bout scaping now but I no ahm the hardest worker of us all sept Pa an ahm tired from the night. I dint sleep too well I had weird dreams. So I side to walk over to Snowys grave an tell him all thats happend. He dont no bout Daisy nearly drowning nor Pa culling me nor all the talk bout tamination an other survivors. Weve got a lot to scuss.

In my head I go thru all the things I want to say to Snowy. I dont only have to member em I have to figure out how I feel bout em. With Pa saving Daisy thats easy but with Alices memrys of befor say or the I-dear of the others not all be-ing dead its mor plex cus I dont truely no if these things are good or bad. Ahd all ways thought we wer the only ones left in the world an no-ing thats possly not trues some how larming an siting at the same time.

All so it curs to me now that theres things I orterve askt Pa that I dint. He wer in a good mood an he probly wunta minded. I orterve askt him bout the boxes I saw in that house in the woods. An the books an wy he dint tell us

84

bout em. An wat are them black windows in the ground. I walk long the rivers edge an past Alices sun flowers jus thinking an thinking till I reach the rocks that go down to the sea.

An thats wen I see it. Its there on top of one of the lowest rocks. A dark marks wat it looks like from up here. Wen I get nearer I see that its two dark marks an closer still I can see wat they are even tho I dont see how they can be. I keep walking fast as I can over the sharp rocks till I come so close my eyes cant possly be seeving me.

Its a pair of boots with socks inside em.

My first thought is they must be Pas an hes been keeping em secret like he did with the house in the woods. But then I look closer an I see the size on the inside tongue an its 10 an Pas a 12. I stare at the boots for some time trying to work out wat they mean. I touch the socks theyre soakt thru an so are the boots. I turn an look all round. I cant see any thing that dont belong there only the rocks an the trees an the sea an a couple shrawking birds.

I leave the boots where they are an walk on looking round but still I cant see any thing. Venturely I give up an take the path that goes to Snowys grave. Its strange but wen I round the corner an enter the spinny wat I see firsts the stone an how the name SNOWYs been rased by the rain. Soon as I see wats nex to the stone the black bird an the berfly start flapping an flying at the same time.

Its a mans body. The mans all mos naked an hes lying on his back his eyes are closed. I-ther hes a sleep or hes dead I dont no which. Slowly quitely I walk over to him an bend down. I touch his shoulder. Its warm.

Sunly his eyes are open.

XIII

He is breathless, his eyes huge, face illuminated with blood and happiness. I try to look surprised, not fearful.

'Pa, Alice, Daisy, come quickly!' Finn calls. 'Listen, there's a stranger, I found him by the shore. Near Snowy's gravestone.'

'What?'

'A man! I found a man, hardly wearing any clothes. He says he swam here! He's hungry and thirsty. Come on, we need to help him.'

The three of us are standing around him now, the girls asking questions, Alice's sceptical, Daisy's irrelevant. Finn grows impatient with them and shouts at me. 'Pa, will you come and help him? He needs something to eat and drink. I think he's had a long journey.' And then, in a softer, pleading voice, 'He seems nice, Pa. I don't think he's contaminated.'

'That's not something you can *see*, Finn. But sure, let's get some food and drink together. You and Alice go first. Me and Daisy'll come after.'

My heart quakes as I say this. Am I making a mistake? But I need time to think.

I ask Finn what he looks like, and he replies, 'Dark-haired, tall like you.'

'Younger than me?'

'I guess so.'

'Stronger than me?'

86

'No. But he looks quite strong. You can see his muscles under his skin, you know.'

'Does he have a gun or a knife or anything?'

'No, nothing. He didn't try to hurt me, Pa. He's nice, honestly.'

'What's his voice like?'

'Not as deep as yours, but it sounds a bit the same. He talks the same language as us! He understood everything I said!'

O mine enemy, hast thou found me?

My heart gallops as I trot slowly alongside Daisy, she carrying a bag of fresh-picked cherries and me a bottle of wine, Goldie running up ahead. A warm little welcoming party. Does he know I tried to kill him, this stranger? Will I see it in his eyes? Or what if he isn't a stranger? Would he say anything to Finn or Alice that might . . . *upset* them? For without are dogs and sorcerers and whosoever loveth and maketh a lie. I carry the hunting knife in the holster inside my vest, just in case. It takes maybe half an hour for us to reach the shore, then I have to help Daisy over the rocks because her legs aren't long enough. From a distance, I hear Goldie bark – once, twice, three times – and then go quiet. Just before we enter the cove, Daisy holds my hand and walks behind me. She's shy, for the first time in her life. I almost laugh.

I don't recognise him instantly. There's a moment when his face is in profile, his left eye covered by a shock of dark hair, and all I really see is his mouth, opening and closing (talking to Finn, who's crouched beside him), and his left hand (patting Goldie, who's curled up at his feet), and his shoulders and chest, which don't have the barrelling girth of mine, have obviously never dug holes for a living, but are also wider, more toned, and lead down to a belly that is all ridges and hollows, not the bulging wineskin that's grown beneath my own pectorals. So my first impressions are envy, dislike, mistrust, and I touch the handle of the hunting knife as he turns, and.

There is a silence, charged, for what feels like a minute but is probably only a second or two, as our eyes meet (we are, I guess, eight or ten feet apart now), before Will smiles, all fake easy charm, and says, 'Finn here was just telling me how you make these delicious pancakes . . .' His voice goes on and I see, from the corner of my eye, his rucksack, black and green, lying in the grass near Snowy's gravestone, and Alice, standing over by the trees, her body tensed, eyes wide, face pale, and Finn, crouched next to him, his face turned, eyes searching mine, excited, expectant, like Goldie when he's caught something, and I say, my voice harsh and sudden,

'Who are you? What are you doing here?'

(Finn looks worried.)

Will goes silent then stands up, smiling (what feeling lies beneath that smile – nervousness? irony? cunning?) and moves a couple feet towards me, his right hand held out. He's maybe two inches taller than me. I stare at his hand (soft skin and dirty fingernails never done a hard day's work in his) as if it's a piece of shit, and he gets the message, lets it fall, and says (mockingly?) respectful, 'Sir, my name's Will and I'm from . . .'

'Babylon.'

'Sorry?'

'You're from the other world, I can hear it in your voice. The world we left behind. The world that got drowned by the flood.'

Silence, the flicker of a frown. 'What . . .'

'Don't you lie to me, boy. You may be young but you're old enough to remember the Great Flood. How did you survive it?'

His mouth opens and closes. 'I, er . . . I guess I was lucky.'

'You certainly were. We built an ark. I knew it was coming, you see, I could read the signs. But anyway . . . we can talk about this later. Finn tells me you're hungry and thirsty?'

'Well, Finn's been kind enough – Alice too – to bring me some food and water already. And . . .'

'I brought you some wine, if you want it. And Daisy here has some cherries. Freshly picked.'

'Daisy? Hi, I'm Will.' Bending down to speak to her, coaxing her out from behind my legs; the blush and smile on her face the fucking bastard if he touches my daughter if he very kind of you I love cherries such a warm welcome I really appreciate on and on the charm so false pouring out his mouth just like his father but more natural better at lying because he doesn't yet have that steel dollared glint in his eyeballs because he's younger and more handsome I want to Alice watching her cheeks ashen horror-struck or and Finn and Daisy eating out his palm the innocents the ignorants after all I told them warned them last night about contamination and here they are I want to wherefore doth the way of the wicked prosper wherefore are all they happy that deal very treacherously pull them out like sheep for the slaughter O Lord and prepare them for the day of.

Will.

My nephew.

Their cousin.

They must neverever

We walk towards the ark. Alice and Goldie have gone on ahead. Daisy holds my hand and looks back over her shoulder as she walks, so she keeps stumbling into me. Finn is behind us, holding hands with Will (the son dishonoureth) as he talks away. I half-listen to his chatter, but it's safe, anodyne, all gollies at the beauty of the island and the books the kids have read and the food we gave him, and I look up at the still-misty sky and remember a harsh blue sky that boiling day in the City of Angels the last time I saw him when was that eight summers ago I'd lost my ad job it was after the earthquake and my so-called nervous breakdown I was working for a firm of swimming-pool builders called Deep Blue Heaven in Christian's garden he'd hired us to construct an infinity pool hired us why us because he was friends with my boss because he wished to humiliate me that summer was one of the hottest on record and this was August we'd been there for weeks every day the same ritual me calling them Mr and Mrs Highfield they treating me just like any other worker on their land because they said they didn't want to embarrass me in front of my colleagues all surly Mexicans and they were right God-damn it which only makes it worse but that day that day Charlotte sorry Mrs Highfield had invited Mary round with the kids because she knew there was no aircon in our apartment (and whose fault was that) and Mary and I had argued at the bottom of the drive hissing almost silently at each other her saying I had a bad attitude a chip on my shoulder and then she'd driven home and I'd gone back to work on my knees tiling in the deep end with Dez Rez or some such shit coming out the radio and then the call for lunch and sitting in the shade of the company truck on the grass eating limp sandwiches and drinking lukewarm water hating Christian knowing my kids were in his living room too shy (or ashamed) to come out and say hello to me with Chloë and Will watching TV and going up to the house to use the bathroom as usual taking off my shoes at the door wiping my hands on my shirt a glance into the living room (Alice and Finn sat either side of Chloë their eyes glued to the screen and Will lounging coolly on the beanbag twelve years old gelled hair earring ironic smirk not looking at me as I pass) and then down the passage to the bathroom long piss wash hands splash face long gulp of water and then out back up the passageway and look at my children see Alice glance up at me then back at the TV the sad glimmer of panic embarrassment on her face and Finn little Finn still a toddler lost in the waves of friendly colour and noise both of them CONTAMINATED and Will fucking Will sitting there in his fucking beanbag in his fucking Lakers T-shirt hands behind his head turning his gaze from the TV to me the cold contempt in his eyes and saying in his polite-to-the-workmen voice Excuse me but my father said you aren't allowed in here and me What the hell are you talking and Will He said it wasn't appropriate for you to come in here and me My own children are and Will He said if you insisted on coming in I was to call my mother and me You can't stop me saying hello to my own and he It's our house and me Come on kids we're going and Finn and Alice looking nervously at Will who'd been Put In Charge and me Forget it and going outside into the heat wrapped in humiliation hating my nephew hating his father hating my own contaminated children and

'Did you really swim all that way?'

Finn's voice shocks me back to Now.

Will begins to say something, but I interrupt. 'What happened to your boat?' I demand, stopping and turning to face him.

'My boat?'

'Don't play the innocent! I saw you, with my binoculars.'

'Oh, you saw me.' For a second the charm drops from his face and he stares coldly into my eyes I want to fucking kill him the fucking but is it already too late the children like him now how can I. 'It sprang a leak. I had to abandon it.'

'So you probably only swam a mile or two?'

'I guess so. Something like that.'

'But Pa, you said that water's . . .'

'Poisoned, yeah. I know, Finn, but if he only swam a couple miles, he might be OK.'

'Might be?'

'Yeah.' The seed of an idea. 'He might be.'

'The water's poisoned?' Will looks at me again, raises an eyebrow. 'I didn't know that.'

'It's common sense surely, after all that's happened.'

'I suppose so. But don't worry Finn, I'm sure your dad's right, a couple miles won't kill me. It's not like I swallowed it or anything.'

We walk back to the ark and drink some mint tea. We eat lunch, but Will says he's not hungry any more, only tired, so I tell him to sleep in my bed. After lunch I go to check on him, and hear his breathing, deep and regular. So I leave the kids to rest in their room and walk back across the island to the cove. Will's rucksack is where he left it, in the shade near the cat's gravestone. I open it up and remove his belongings one by one. Clothes, suncream, biscuits, a bottle, a sleeping bag, a hunting knife. I take the last of these and stuff everything else back into the bag. He'll know I've been through his stuff, but I don't care. In fact I want him to know. This is MY island and MY laws apply.

On the way back I think through all the ways I might kill him. A shooting accident in the forest. A snake in his sleeping bag. Crushed rat poison in his wine. A quiet strangling at night. An accidental fall from a treetop. But each time some voice inside me says it's too late, I already missed my chance. If I couldn't shoot him when he was a mere dark mark in the distance, anonymous, not even human, how can I possibly do it now? How can I kill him? My own flesh and blood. But what if he.

Fuck O fuck what a fucking mess.

Back in the ark, Finn's awake, but all the rest are asleep. Finn begins asking me questions, but I tell him I'm tired and go to lie down in his bed. I don't intend to sleep – I intend to listen out for the click and creak of my bedroom door, the sound of Will's voice – but fatigue steals over me in the gently wheezing dimness and I.

When I wake my mouth's dry and tastes bitter. The other two beds are empty. Panicked, I sit up and walk to the door. There, I stand, fingers poised on the handle, ear to the wood, listening. Their voices are quite loud; they must be in the living room.

(FINN: '. . . you come from, Will?'

WILL: 'It's nothing like this place, that's for sure. It's so beautiful here, so peaceful.'

DAISY: 'Are there very tall houses where you come from?'

WILL: 'There sure are. Buildings taller than the tallest tree you ever saw, Daisy. We call them skyscrapers.'

FINN: 'But didn't they all get destroyed in the flood?'
WILL: 'Well . . . not all of them.'
FINN: 'What about cars, are there still . . .')

I open the door and say loudly, 'Wow, I didn't realise I was so tired.'

Will, who was sitting in the armchair with Daisy and Finn one on each arm, jumps up apologetically and says something about me obviously needing the sleep. It's nearly evening, I can tell from the colour of the light coming through the porthole. 'What have you all been talking about?'

'Will was telling us about where he comes from,' Finn volunteers.

Will blushes. 'Yeah, and before that, Finn was telling me about all the work you guys do here: milking the goats and digging fields and chopping down trees and so on. It was fascinating.'

I stare into his eyes as he talks. Woe unto them that call evil good, and good evil. He meets my gaze for a few beats, then looks away, uncomfortable. But, as Daisy and Finn start to chatter at the same time, their words colliding, I understand that Will has not contaminated them. Not yet. And I breathe out relief through my mouth.

The evening passes without damage. We eat outside, under the branch roof, and then I get Alice (who's sulky and hostile for some reason) to play the violin. After that, I put the children to bed, close the door of the living room, and sit down across from Will, each of us with a glass of wine.

'It's been a long time since we last saw each other, Will.'

'Yes, it certainly has.'

'And it'll be even longer before we see each other again.'

'Pardon me?'

'I want you to leave tomorrow morning, early. And never come back.'

I watch his face as I speak: a soft frown; the smile curdling, pursing: an expression that signals not shock, but only mild disappointment.

'I'm afraid I won't be able to do that.'

The slight tremble of nerves in his voice. I stroke the clasp of my hunting knife.

'Would you care to tell me why not?'

'Well, for a start, I don't have a boat any more. You can hardly expect me to swim all the way back, can you? I mean, if the water's poisoned . . .'

We look in each other's eyes for several moments. He doesn't smile or look away. It's like we're arm-wrestling, and I've tried a couple pushes, only to discover my opponent is stronger, much stronger, than I'd imagined. And so far, he hasn't pushed back.

'That's true,' I say.

He leans back in his chair. 'This is a beautiful island. I'd like to stay a little longer . . . with your permission.'

'While you build yourself a boat?'

'Sure. I imagine it'll be done before the end of the summer.'

'Long before, I'd have thought.'

'Well . . . I have to get it right. Make sure it doesn't have any leaks this time.'

'Yes, I suppose that makes sense.'

'Your children seem very happy and healthy. They're great kids. You must be proud . . .'

You do anything to my children you fuck and I'll fucking.

'I am.'

There's a silence. I drink some wine. I hear him sigh, breathe in, and then:

'My father didn't send me, you know.'

'I didn't say he did.'

'I know, I just . . . thought you'd like to know.'

I nod, slowly. 'How *is* your father?'

'He hasn't changed.' A trace of bitterness? 'I have, though.'

'Naturally. You were only, what, twelve, when I last saw you. It would be strange if you hadn't changed.'

'That's right. Only twelve. It seems even longer ago than that somehow . . .'

'Yeah. Another world. The flood changed everything, of course. No one could go through that and still be the same person. Except for the children. They were so young, you know. Finn and Daisy, they don't remember the world before the flood at all. And Alice . . . well, she's got a few memories, but nothing very solid. I think it would be better if you didn't talk to them about it – about the world you come from. I fear it would disturb them.'

'Right.' He nods. 'I understand.' Then, swallowing, leaning forward, he says, 'So . . . tell me what happened to you and your family during the flood. I don't actually remember it too well myself, to be honest with you. You say you knew it was coming?'

'Yes, Will, I knew.'

And I tell him the story.

I tell him the story, from beginning to end.

I tell him about the Year of Disasters and that evening, soon after Daisy's birth, when I sat with Mary, watching TV, and the President came on screen to warn us that a war might be coming, a war he wished to avoid, but would not back down from if the other side did not see reason. And how I didn't even feel the old hatred for him any more because I could see God through the lightwaves and the pixels, I could see the catastrophe that was yet to come, the Great Wave. And I tell him how Mary and I sat on the couch, holding each other close, images of death and disaster blinking from the TV screen and flashing in the silent tears that rolled down Mary's face, and how God spoke to me through the hissing baby monitor, He said the end of all flesh is come before me, for the earth is filled with violence, and behold I will destroy them. Behold I, even I, do bring a flood of waters upon the earth, to destroy all flesh, wherein is the breath of life, and everything upon the earth shall die, all but YOU. And how the next day I went to the hardware store and bought all the wood they had, and I went to the library and borrowed a book called *How to Build an Ark*, and I set to work in the back garden of our Crenshaw apartment. How I stopped turning up for work because I knew money would soon lose its value, would mean nothing, and how I stayed at home in the garden, sawing and measuring and hammering and sanding and varnishing for four hundred days and four hundred nights until finally the ark was ready, and how everyone neighbours colleagues family everyone thought I was crazy because they did not see what I saw they could not hear what I heard everyone yes even my wife believed I was wrong wrong in the head and but I KNEW that the Wave was coming and on the night when the storm began and the heavens opened Mary believed me then O yes and she followed me and the children and animals into the ark and we sealed up the door as the rains fell upon the earth and the waters rose and the thunder roared and the lightning flashed brighter than the sun illuminating horrors I saw trees and hills crawling with people all of them pushing and crushing the weakest to save themselves the cowards but IN VAIN for the waters were rising ever higher and the naysayers knew in their hearts that I had been right after all and their lives were ending now they were dying arms upraised to the sky faces disappearing under water and we watched through the portholes as Babylon fell and became the habitation of devils and how we sailed for many days and how Mary died saving baby Daisy from the waves and how we finally sighted land and made our home here here on this blessed island and how the world beyond these shores is CONTAMINATED and I will not let anything or anyone touch or harm my children for if he did I would KILL him I would SMITE him I would GRIND YOU INTO DUST YOU FUCKING do you understand me do you understand what I'm saying and he says yes yes I understand.

His face's white and his eyes are wide and he says he understands.

Yes, yes. Everything's going to be all right.

He understands.

XIV

Its go-ing to be a nother flamer of a day I can tell. But erly morning here in the shade of the Afterwoods the grounds still damp an cool. It raind last night like its raind nearly evry night since He came. Pa said the other day its like a mirror cull. No rain for moons an moons an then the great storm an His coming an ever since the night rain filling the lake an feeding the tatoes an matoes an melons an strawbrees an keeping the river all clear an deep an I-see cold.

I hant askt Pa if Hes an angel sent by God but I reckon He must be. Weare all happy an saved since He came afterall. Even Daisy who wer shy an fraid of Him to gin with. Even Goldy who barkt an wer spicious of Him. Even Pa who reckond Will wer taminated wen he rived an spoke real dark an force full to Him an crusht his Devil on the ground. Even Alice who wer cold an weird to Him for days an days even she seems happy now an smiles wen ever she sees Him. No there int any of us who dont like Will.

I walk thru the long grass barefoot so I can feel the damp erth on my soles. My trainers are tied by ther laces round my neck. Ahm on my way to Wills shelter so we can talk like all ways an side wat we need to do this morning. The last few days weve been sawing an stacking firewood for the winter. Theres a massive pile of it now by the river behind Alices field of sun flowers. If you climb up an stand on top of it you can see over the sun flowers heads to the grass tween them an the Afterwoods.

Befor that I helpt Will make His shelter. We made it from willow branches an tar porlin. Inside its not big but its cool an the rain slides off it wen it falls at night. Wen it wer finisht Will thankt me for all my help but He dint have to cus I joyd it I joy jus be-ing with Him an us do-ing stuff to gether. He said ahm the hardest worker Hes ever met. The berfly seemd to grow inside me wen He said that. Ahm thinking maybe we shud dig a nother field of tatoes this morning cus weare eating more of em now Wills here. Pa cud even help us if hes not busy in the Afterwoods. An then after the noon sleep we can go hunt-ing like mos ways. We shot a deer a wile back. Pa made a stew from it an we ate it for days.

I come out from the first line of trees an into the sun so I can check the traps in the long grass. I stop an put my trainers on first tho case I get trapt my self. With a dead branch I push the long grass out the way. The first ones emty an sos the second but wen I come to the third I dont need to push the grass out the way cus its all ready flat-tend in a half circle round the trap an I can hear a noise like Goldy makes in his sleep wen hes having bad dreams. I slow down an hold my breth as I draw closer. The memry of Snowys stiff body flashes in my mind. The duum duums loud in my ears.

Wat is it.

Wen ahm standing bove it I let my breth out an the duum duums quite down. Its only a rabbit. Poor things still a live tho thrashing an nawing its leg caught an bloody in the steel mouth. It shakes like crazy for a couple moments then lies down like its dead for a few mor. My two eyes look into its one blackun wen its calm an I feel like I can read its thoughts. Ahm hurting its eye says Let me go. I wonder wat it means at first cus it cunt run far with its leg smasht but then I stand that Let me go means Put me out my misry. It means Kill me please. Ive got a hunting nife hanging on my belt but wen I take it out an look at the blade an think bout slitting the rabbits neck I can feel the black bird flapping inside me. Wat am I fraid of. Ive cut up rabbits hunerds of times befor. But theyve all ways been dead hant they. Pas all ways kild em. Some thing bout the I-dear of sliding the nife in a throat thats pulsing breathing tensing makes me feel sick an weak an I cant do it.

I side to go an ask Will to put the rabbit out its misry so I tell it ahm sorry an run thru the grass. Its hot in the sun an swets poring out my skin wen I rive at the rocks. I scramble cross em an run into the spinny calling His name. His head comes out the door of the shelter an He blinks at me smiling.

Hey Finn your erly. Wats up.

I splain bout the rabbit wile He crawls out the shelter an rubs his eyes in the sun light.

Will you come I ask. Will you put it out its misry.

Sure Finn he calms.

We run side by side our long shadows spearing into the shade of the Afterwoods. I stop wen we get to the trap with the flattend grass an Will stands beside me looking down at the rabbit but its eyes gon dull. I stare breth held an wait for it to thrash an squeal a gen but its.

Finn He gentles. I think.

I no I say. Weare too late.

He reaches a hand down an touches the rabbits throat.

Yeh ahm fraid so. It musta died wile you wer a way.

I swallow. Ahm so sorry lil rabbit.

Ahm shure it dint suffer long Finn. You ran fast as you cud.

I shudve kild it wen it askt me. I shudve put it out its misry. But I was too weak too.

Will puts a hand on my shoulder an says Dont be so hard on yer self Finn Ikerd never have don that wen I wer yer age.

Truely I ask. I look in His eyes. He dont look a way like Pa some times does.

Truely He plies. Your way stronger an more mature than I wer. Youll be a fine man one day.

The berflys normous inside me.

He bends down an leases the mouth of the trap. Then He lifts the rabbits body up by its ears. Its jus dead now. Its jus a dead rabbit.

An at least weve got our meat for the day He says. We wont need to go out hunting this after noon.

Whatll we do then I ask an straighter way start magining new splorations of the I-land showing Will all the secret places I no. Or maybe we cud go to the lake an He cud teach me how to swim.

Finn listen. His voices strange.

Wat.

Ahm not coming with you this after noon.

Wy.

Cus I told Alice ahd spend some time with her.

Alice. A gen.

Wy I peat.

Cus I promist.

I shrug Okay an He puts an arm round my neck. Your not mad with me he asks.

Course not I say but my voices cold an emty. I dont mean to hurt Him but I cant help it ahm so spointed. Hes been with Alice half our after noons lately.

Pa cuts the rabbit up an lets it stew on the range wile we dig a new field. We wash in the lake an eat the stew an then go to our beds. Wen the suns over head its too hot to do any thing but sleep. Lying in the warm thick dim ness of our room I ask Alice wy she keeps taking Will a way from me. She dint even like Him befor.

Weare going for a walk thats all she plies in a bord sleepy voice.

Can I come.

No.

Wy cant I.

Cus we want to spend some time to gether. A lone to gether.

You do you mean.

We both do.

I dont be leave you I hiss. Hed rather splore the I-land with me Hes jus be-ing kind to you.

She laffs quitely in her throat an sighs Oh Finn.

Wats that sposed to mean.

Such innocents. You have no I-dear.

I dont be leave you I mutter into the pillow. An lie there breathing the bluegrey air till I fall a sleep.

I wake up befor her an drink some water in the kitchen then I go outside. The heats like a wall. Sluggish an weary I go to the river an fill the emty boll. Then I carry it back to the ark. On my way back I see Alice go-ing the other way. Her hair looks difrant an shes wearing a clean wite dress. Theres like red paint or blood on her lips. She looks nice.

I keep on walking to the ark but wen I get there I dont go inside. I stay hidden behind the corner an watch her grow smaller thru the gardens an venturely spear into the corn. I take a mouth full from the boll and follow her.

Inside the corn its dark an the grounds pitted where the plows been. I keep tripping up an the corn leaves scratch my face. Wen I come out I blink in the dazzle then I see her up a head go-ing round the lake. I guess she must be walking to Wills shelter so I side to take the short cut an beat her there.

A long the river bank I run. Past the wood pile an on till I reach the rocks. Wen I get level with the long grass near the Afterwoods I look to see if shes there but the views emty. On I go till I reach the spinny an then silently slide in tween the trees. Waiting. Watching. After a wile I hold my breth an creep tords Wills shelter. Lissning.

Duum duum. Birdsong. Cadanoise.

I open the door of the shelter an look inside. Dark emty ness. I make a V with my brow. If theyre not here where are they.

I rush back out the spinny an clamber back over the rocks till I reach the long grass. No thing on the rising.

I walk tords the lake but half way past Alices field I hear a strange sound that makes me stop an listen. Wat wer it. I close my eyes an hold my breth.

Lafter. Thats wat it wer. I hear it a gen from some where to my right. Lafter an. Like breathing or moaning. Like some body whos tasted nice food. Saying Mmmm.

I turn to my right an see the sun flowers. They all stare back at me like Who are you. Like Wat are you looking at. Maybe its cus theyre Alices I dont no but I kinda feel like theyre guarding the field like they dont want to let me in.

I stand there for a wile lissning to the lafter an quite talk an Mmmm-ing and then I side wat to do.

I walk round the sun flowers till I get to the wood pile an climb up on top. From there I can see the long grass at the other side where Ive jus been standing an I can see tween the rows of sun flowers I can see the dry erth an I can see.

Them.

Him an her.

Wat are they do-ing.

Ther faces keep moving close to gether like they want to whisper to each other but they dont put ther lips to each others ears they put em to each others lips. Like theyre talking into each others mouths. Like theyre kissing good night but the kisses last too long ther lips stay to gether for duum duum duum duum duum duum duum duum duum duum duum duum duum duum duum duum duum duum. An then ther lips part an they laf an I let my breth out.

Wat are they do-ing.

Its some thing bad I think. Its some thing they shunt be do-ing.

Theyre kissing a gen now I lose count of the duum duums. An now Hes sliding the straps of her dress down her arms an I can see her chest that I used to see all the time but now she gets barrast if ahm there wen shes dressing. It used to be flat an brown like mine but now its like two wite lil udders an Hes touching it with his hands. Is he milking her. She says Mmmm. Theyre eating each others mouths now an theyre lying on the ground. Her dressll get dirty. He takes off his T-shirt an his backs brown you can see the muscles under the skin. Watching em I keep having to mind my self to breath. I feel guilty an look a way but then I want to see wat theyre do-ing so I look a gen an His mouths on her chest. Its weird is he sucking her milk or wat are they wat are they do-ing.

Some thing bad.

Some thing they shunt be do-ing.

Maybe its the Devil thats temted em.

I side to stop em. Maybe I can save em from the bad thing an theyll say thank you to me wen theyre free of the Devils spell. I climb down off the wood pile an walk tords the sun flowers. I cant see em now but I no where they are. An I can hear em. Breathing. Going Mmmm.

Sunly I start running ahm angry an sad an even thru the heat I run fast as I can. I need to put em out ther misry.

The sun flowers are looking the other way so they cant stop me now. I run thru two rows of em an see Will an Alice in front of me an I scream Stop it. Stop it. Stop it. Stop it. Stop it.

Nex thing I no Alices standing in front of me. Her hands are pulling up her dress an her faces red shes staring at me with I-scold hate. Shes talking hissing at me I listen to the words wats she saying.

the hell you think your do-ing Finn. Wy did you follow us. Say some thing.

I wanted to no wat you wer do-ing.

An now you no.

Yeh. An its rong.

No its not.

Its bad wat your do-ing.

How wud you no. You dont no any thing.

You dint even like Him befor.

Well I do now so go.

He wer my friend I say.

The tears are coming up my throat now an trying to squeeze in the backs of my eyes. I can hear em in my voice.

He wer my friend not yours. Wyd you have to steal Him from me.

I dint steal Him. He likes me too thats all.

You all ways have to ruin things for me. All ways. Wy cant you let me be happy. Wy

But the tears have scaped now an theyre poring out my eyes. I put my hands over my eyes so all I sees red an black. The harder I press the blacker it goes. I feel like ahm swaying.

Go away Finn I hear her say.

I gin to walk tho I dont no where ahm go-ing.

XV

Walking in the garden in the cool of the shade, here by the edge of the lake. It's late afternoon, and I've just woken up. Over the water the heat haze flickers, but here between birch trees a breeze blows across my face. I hear birdsong and the river, His voice as the sound of many waters . . .

Everything's too good to be true. Ergo it must be false. I know this, and it is why I guard my suspicions tight and dark inside me, always smiling and pretending, like he does.

Yesterday was a moonday, so it has been twenty-nine days since Will landed on our island, and during that time it has rained almost every night. The lake is full, the river high, the horizon invisible. Since he came, Alice has been kind, cheerful and polite towards me; she is a changed girl. Finn and Daisy love him, of course. And the work he does, the respect he shows . . . And yet I know I must stay vigilant. Will is a charmer, he's a snake. I must not let him hypnotise me with his words, smiles, actions. There are hours, whole days, when I wish I could just relax and enjoy these moments, this sense of security, like my children do. But I am here to protect them, and I must not let my guard down. What is he up to? What does he WANT?

Only once that I know of has he spoken a word out of place, back on the second day. Finn was asking him about televisions and telephones, and Will took out his mobile. This was outside, under the branch roof, and I was tending the vines, watching from the corner of my eye. When I saw Finn take that evil instrument in his hands, I yelled 'No' and ran towards them as Finn put the tiny plastic Devil to his ear. Will saw the look on my face and took his Devil away from Finn, who cried out. 'It doesn't work,' said Will, to me, fear in his voice. 'There's no signal up here. Listen.' He handed It to me and I let It fall to the hard ground. There, like a shiny beetle, I crushed it beneath the heel of my boot. Finn shouted 'Why?' and I told him about the microwaves, the toxins, the radiation pouring from the Devil into his ear. Finn stared at Will, who said 'I'm sorry, I'm sorry, I wasn't thinking.' Finn didn't speak for the rest of that day.

On I walk, round the edge of the lake. I left Daisy playing with Goldie in the shade behind the ark. Finn, I guess, is somewhere with Will, as always. As for Alice . . . down by the beach? I don't know. Not so long ago, the dark emptiness of that not knowing would have bred horrors in my mind; I would have visioned her entering the Afterwoods, seeking out secrets, but now she seems to have forgotten those obsessions. I have followed her several times, unknown to her, but she never even went near the forest, only dreamily drew symbols in the sand or read Shakespeare or stared out to sea, her eyes filled not with longing but with tranquillity. Sometimes, to my astonishment, she watered her field of sunflowers, in the evening, when she was free to do as she wished and her work for the day was done. I have never known Alice like this before. It is as if, before my very eyes, she is turning from a girl into a woman.

I do not trust him as far as I can spit. And yet, I cannot deny the harmony that exists now between me and my children. O Lord, I am grateful for that small mercy.

I walk slowly towards the river, past the huge woodpile that Will sawed and stacked, and along the riverbank to the southern shore, where he has built his shelter. There's something I want to talk to him about. I clamber over the rocks, thinking about how I will begin this conversation. Then, drawing near to the spinny of trees, I hear sobbing. The sound of a small child.

I tense. 'Daisy? Finn?'

I enter the spinny and see my son sitting in the shade by Snowy's gravestone, elbows on knees and face in hands, tears rolling between his fingers.

'Finn, what's the matter?'

He looks up, then covers his eyes again.

'Why are you crying?'

I put my arms round his shoulders and feel them heave as another gust of sobs pours out of him.

'Finn . . . please. Tell me what's wrong. Are you hurt?'

'N-no. I'm . . .'

I pull his hands from his face and wipe his tears with the hem of my T-shirt. And I shall wipe away all tears from their eyes, and there shall be no more sorrow, nor crying, neither shall there be any more pain. His sobbing slows down, grows quieter. I rub his back. 'It's all right, Finn. Now tell me. What's happened? Why are you upset?'

'It's Alice,' he says dully, staring at the ground. 'She's stolen him from me.'

'I don't understand. Stolen who?'

'Will, of course. He was my friend, and now he's hers. Just because she's . . .'

'Finn, Finn, calm down. Why can't you both be friends with Will?'

'He doesn't care about me any more, and it's her fault. All he cares about is her because she's . . .'

Thy sister came with subtilty, and hath taken away thy blessing.

He goes silent. I frown. 'Because she's what?'

He looks up at me with something like guilt on his face.

'Because she's a girl,' he mumbles.

A tightening in my chest. 'What do you mean?'

'*You* know. They're kissing and wrestling and laughing and . . . breathing funny all the time.'

Finn's face has gone red.

'Kissing? You mean . . . on the mouth?'

'Like they're eating each other's faces.'

And to think I almost trusted that snake. Almost believed his lies.

'Are they kissing now, Finn?'

He shrugs. 'Probably. They were before. Rolling around naked on the ground.'

Naked.

'WHERE ARE THEY?'

Finn looks very small and frightened suddenly.

I lower my voice, ask again, 'Where are they? Do you know where they are?'

'In the sunflowers,' he replies in a small voice.

I stand up. 'Thank you, Finn.'

You are my beloved son, in whom I am well pleased.

A nervous smile flickers across his face. 'What are you going to do . . . to them?'

'Nothing. Go back to the ark.'

I begin to walk away.

'Pa . . . is it bad, what they're doing?'

I turn around – 'The ark, Finn' – and start running towards the sunflower field.

Kissing and wrestling and breathing funny. He might be wrong. He might not have seen what he thinks he's seen. Kissing and laughing and rolling around naked. Finn might be making it up because he's jealous. He could be lying exaggerating I must stay calm. Wait and see what. The edges of my vision are reddening as I run. I slow down, take deep breaths, and the crimson fades. I stop, close my eyes, open them again, look around: green trees, blue sky, yellow and black sunflowers. Calm, stay calm, you know what happens when you. At an easy pace I move forward. And they heard the voice of the Father walking in the garden in the cool of the day, and Will and Alice hid themselves from the presence of the Father amongst the trees of the garden. And the Father called unto. But no, I keep silent, and walk on, until I reach the sunflowers. I stand at the edge of Alice's field and stare at the identical faces. The black circles at the centre of each look suddenly like mouths open screaming in horror. Calm down, calm. Innocent till proven guilty. I hear muffled laughter from somewhere among the screaming flowers, and walk along the rows, staring down each in turn. Innocent till proven GUILTY. And I shall rule them with a rod of iron; as the vessels of a potter shall they be broken to shivers, even as I received of my Father. Along the rows, one by one: empty, empty, empty, empty, stop. A pair of feet, naked? I move to the next row and see a tangle of flesh in the baking hazing shadowy distance. I blink, squint, sweat stings my eye. Maybe I'm just imagining the edges of the field turn red like blood and I calm down, calm. Revenge is best served cold. I close my eyes, breathe slowly, but my heart won't listen to reason. CONTAMINATED. And first I will recompense their iniquity and their sin double, because they have defiled my land, they have filled mine inheritance with the carcasses of their abominable deeds. I move through the sunflowers, their silent screaming heads. Walking in the garden in the heat of the day. I hear laughter again, and then Mmmm. BETRAYED. I will cause them to know mine hand and my might, and they shall know my name is. Touch my daughter and I'll fucking kill you you fucking. *Calm*. But the red at the edges is growing inward, like a bloodstain spreading, blotting out all other colours. The sunflowers like screaming bloodheads. I shade my eyes and look at their bodies half-naked entangled in the dry soil, black lines on their skin from the sunflowers' shadows. I can't see their heads or feet only their torsos and their thighs and. RUINED. Barren hate, sour-eyed disdain and discord shall bestrew the union of your bed with weeds so loathly that you shall hate it both. I stand, frozen, in the broiling sunlight. I cannot move or speak. Their bodies are turning red, their skin glazed with blood. Let mine eyes run down with tears night and day, and let them not cease, for my virgin daughter is broken with a great breach, O with a very grievous blow. And the Father said to Alice, WHAT IS THIS THAT THOU HAST DONE? I take another step forward I am going to fucking kill you and then I can feel it. That weird flutter in my chest like I've disturbed a nest of wasps. And their bodies slick with blood with sweat with writhing. I want to shout out but my voice is weak as a dreamer's in my throat and the red earth's spinning my legs melt I fall. And the soil dry in my fingers on my face in my mouth the taste of it.

I open my eyes. I cannot move or speak. I am paralysed. O Lord give me strength. Am I dying?

I lie in the grass like a deadman and lift my eyes up, past the sunflowers, to the sky. I stare into the pitiless blue. I stare into the face of God. I cry unto thee, and thou dost not hear me. Thou art become cruel to me. With thy strong hand, thou opposest thyself against me. Thou liftest me up to the wind; thou causest me to ride upon it, and dissolvest my substance. Tears escape my eyes as the blue sky rolls on overhead, dazzling and indifferent.

XVI

Ahm sat nex to his grave stone trying to find the words to tell him evry thing thats happend. Its so long since I talkt to Snowy. Ever since Will rived at the I-land Ive glected him. In truth ahd all mos forgot his grave wer here. Jus cus Wills shelter wer all I saw wen I came to this spinny. Poor Snowy.

Ahm sorry I forgot you Snowy. You wer a true friend you never bandond me. I love you Snowy an ahm sorry I hant been here to talk to you for a longtime. Wats been happning since the last time I wer here. Too many things to scribe ahm fraid. Evry things changed an changed a gen. I wer sad and then I wer happy an now ahm sad a gen. Cus shes stolen Him from me.

I hate her.

Ahm sorry Snowy I no I shunt say bad things like that but I do I truely hate her. I wish she wer dead an I cud be like brothers with Will a gen or.

Or he cud be like a father to me.

Yeh cus thats how I felt int it. Like Pa dint matter any mor. Like he wer kinda faded shaded in the blazing light that came from Will.

Ahm sorry Pa ahm sorry Snowy cus you wer the ones who loved me not Him.

The tears come up my throat an into my mouth an the backs of my eyes like they did befor Pa came an found me here. I told him wat ahd seen an now hes gon to search for em. For Will an Alice. Pa lookt real angry wen I told him. Angriern Ive ever seen him. It must be bad wat they did. Wat theyre do-ing. I wunt like to be in ther shoes wen he finds em.

Ahm thirsty a gen. I look round for the boll of water but it int here I musta left it by the river. So I walk back slowly thru the heat thinking bout all thats happened today an watll happen wen Pa finds Will an Alice. I mag-ine em be-ing wipt or banisht from the I-land floating a way on a raft like the one in the Tales yelling how theyre sorry an us noring ther cries watching em slowly spearing into the rising.

At the river I find the boll an fill it with I-see water. I drink it down then fill it a gen. Ahm on my way back to the ark wen it curs to me to climb the wood pile. Jus to see wat I can see. I clamber on top an look over the sun flowers an.

There they are.

A gen.

I cant be leave it.

Him an her culling an kissing an rubbing each others skin like befor. His muscly back an her lil wite udders. The black strypt shadows on ther skin. But wheres Pa. He went to find em I tol him they wer here an now.

Some thing catches my eye further a head in the long grass at the other side of the field. Some thing blue on the ground. I squint thru the dazzle an see its a body. Some body. That blue shirt. Its Pa. Lying down in the long grass. Is he a sleep or.

Sunly Ive jumpt off the wood pile an ahm sprinting round the sun flower field yelling Pa Pa Pa. Fast as I can till I get to his body. I lean over him an look down. I cant see his face its looking in the erth an his legs are all twisted under him. His body in the long grass minds me of the rabbit this morning. But Pa int thrashing. Hes not moving a tall. He musta had one of his heart aches.

Duum duum duum duum. I can feel my own heart ache.

Pas not go-ing to die I tell my self calm down but the panics spurting out my mouth in yells an gasps.

Ohnoohnoohno wat if hes dead like Snowy. Wat if I can never talk to him a gen. Wat if hes left us for ever an weare all a lone on the I-land.

Ahm so scared I cant move.

Alice comes out the sun flowers with narrowd eyes an sees Pa lying in the grass.

Oh. Is he.

She sorta smiles an sunly ahm fild with rage. You did this I cuse her. You gave him a heart ache.

No I dint wat do you.

He musta seen you. You an Him do-ing wat you wer do-ing. I new it wer bad. Pa wer coming to punish you but he. He musta.

Will comes out the sun flowers an asks us wats rong.

Alice says Its my father. I think hes.

Will neels down nex to Pa an touches his neck. Jus like he did with the rabbit.

Ohnoohnoohno.

Will looks up at Alice an then me. Hes a live dont worry. Pass me your boll Finn.

I look down in my hand an see the boll of water there. I dint even no ahd carried it with me. I give it to Will an he pors some over Pas face.

Theres a sort of lil groan.

Pa.

Alice go an pare some food for him. Soup or.

Theres rabbit stew I say. On the range.

Perfect says Will. Alice runs off tords the ark.

He pors some mor water. Rubs Pas face with his hand.

Pa groans a gen louder.

Finn has any thing like this happend befor.

Yeh its his heart. It aches some times.

Has he clapsed like this befor.

Once. He got better tho.

I crouch down nex to Will my heart still going Duum Duum Duum Duum an watch Pas face as Will pors mor water on it. Wills holding his face off the ground. His mouth opens an closes an he makes a nother lil noise.

Pa.

Slowly his eyes open.

Will says Can you hear me. How are you feeling.

Pa opens his mouth a gen but no sound comes out. Will lifts Pas body up so hes sitting an then puts the boll of water to his lips. Pa drinks some. He coffs an then drinks some mor.

Hes a live. I feel so leaved Ikerd all mos float a way.

Pa did you have one of yer heart aches.

Yeh Finn I think so he plies. His voices rusty like he hant used it for moons.

Your not go-ing to die are you Pa.

He smiles a lil. No Finn ahm go-ing to be fine.

We shud get him out the sun says Will. Do you think you can stand.

Pa tries to get up but hes too weak. Its like wen hes drunk but I no hes not. I hold his hand. He looks so old sunly.

Ahl carry him to the ark Will says an He lifts Pas body up on his shoulders. We walk like that Will carrying Pa an me go-ing long beside em watching Pas face. Poor Pa he wer all ways so strong befor an now hes even weakern me.

Wen we get back I feed Pa the stew with a spoon an then me an Will put him in bed. His faces grey an his eyes are yellow streakt with red. His breth smells rotten. I hold his hand it dont spond wen I squeeze it. Daisy comes in an reads him a Tale. Its the one bout the lil boy made of wood whos naughty an a liar an gives his father torments but in the end he lerns to tell the truth an be good an he saves his poor old father.

Pa falls a sleep befor the end of the story. He never gets to hear the happy everafter.

PART TWO

But of the tree of the knowledge of good
and evil, thou shalt not eat of it: for in the
day that thou eatest thereof thou shalt
surely die.

Genesis 2 : 17

XVII

I dreamt that he was gone again – the island was grey, the sea empty, my brother's and father's faces mocked me with their pitying smiles – and I woke with a whispered scream. Now I stare out through the porthole to the starry black beyond, unable to quell the pounding of my heart. What if it were true? This fear is like a poison: I sweat and shake. But no, he would not leave me so, without even a word, a farewell kiss. These nightmares of mine slander him; he is, above all, my friend, despite what my father may claim.

I will sleep no more tonight. I am wide awake, and besides, I think I discern the faintest of glimmers in the sable stillness outside. I hold my breath and peer through the ghostly reflection. Is it that dark hour just before dawn or still the heavy middle of the night? I cannot tell, but I have only to wait. Like the sound an owl makes: to wait, to wait, to woo.

Amid sunflowers, in the shadows of

I shiver, and pull the blanket more tightly around my bare shoulders. Was it really only yesterday that I found out the truth? That oh so hot afternoon, in the sheltered sanctuary of my field, when he said that she was. But overnight the mercury has plunged, and summer's end feels suddenly close. By the next moonday, I fear, the leaves will have begun turning colour – yellow, orange, blood-red, purple, like a bruise in reverse – and then they will fall and he will be gone. He told me so himself, when he first came. Back then, it seemed an age away, but now . . . Oh, stop these dismal thoughts, Alice! There is hope yet. Meet me here at dawn he said, here by our pine

Why? You're not

There's something I have to tell you

More than you've already told me?

Or show you, rather. Meet me here and all will be revealed, I promise

But

Alice I can't say any more now. Just be here

I will

I will, Will, I will. Will will fulfil the treasure of my love. And Will to boot, and Will in overplus. *Amid sunflowers, in the shadows cast by their stalks and heads, the air was cooler and* And then I love thee for thy name is Will.

Retreating from the window, I reach for the box of matches under my bed. Softly, softly, I scrape the scarlet head along the sandpaper. The match flares and, cupping the flame with my other hand, I hold it to the candle's wick. It takes, and I blow out the match flame (that sweet smoke scent) then quickly dress in the dim halo of light. Will's jeans, the belt tightened to keep them on my hips, the bottoms rolled up. One of my mother's old T-shirts: I ♡ L.A. My father doesn't like it when I wear her clothes.

air was cooler and I was wearing my mother's white dress. You look beautiful, he told me, like a lady. I looked down and saw I'd got soil stains on the hem. Damn it, I hissed. Here he said voice low let me

I go through to the kitchen. Putting the candle down on the table, I walk slowly round the room, letting my fingers slide over objects in the half-dark: the smooth metal range, the cold stone slippery jug, the ripe fleshy grapes and tomatoes, the furred skins of peaches and the ridged skins of cucumbers. I feel I am saying farewell to these things, to this room, and yet I do not know why that should be so. Or I do, yet dare not speak it even to myself, for what if it isn't true? What if I only dreamed it?

Amid sunflowers, in the shadow of their stalks and heads, he said that she was

I have told the spy and the tyrant that there are pictures of her in my head, that I remember her – in the world of before and here on this island – but memory is treacherous. The more I seek these images, the more they seem to dissolve. The closer I look, the vaguer they grow. Until I wonder if I truly remember anything at all. Perhaps the spy is right and they are mere phantasms of my imagining, my desire? And yet, when I surprise the memories, when I catch them aslant from the corner of my mind's eye, when they come unbidden at some scent or particular shade of sunlight, I feel sure there is something real there, something uneroded by time. My mother. Where is she now? Under the endless sea or. My heart flutters as the hope rises again inside me, almost more unbearable than the fear.

I feel

I feel as if something precious has been stolen from my life. And I can't even remember what it is.

I walk outside. The air is cold. I look up into the dark bowl of sky, like a sea suspended above us. Several stars I count, and then beyond them, between them, the longer I stare, the more of their cousins I seem to detect, stars and stars and stars, reaching out into infinity, until

I am dizzy at the thought of them, each a sun, with worlds orbiting its blaze, and on each world perchance a million islands in the vast globe-drowning sea, and on none of these, we are meant to believe, another living soul? The whole unimaginably grand universe, and we all alone!

there's a man said Finn a stranger I found him by the shore I don't know how he got there he says he swam said Finn he's thirsty and hungry come on we've got to save him

It was the day after the tempest. The day after the tyrant had told me my memories were contaminated. I followed my brother as he ran, he carrying two bottles of water, I some dried figs and pancakes. Finn ran so fast, his bare brown feet scuttering over grass and rocks, that I was out of breath by the time we reached the shore

How did he even get this far if he was so thirsty and tired?

I told you, he swam

Swam?

The rocks were sharp. They hurt my soles

But

We scrambled over another boulder and Finn pointed down to a stretch of whitish sand. Close to the flat, poisonous sea were a pair of men's boots with red socks hanging out their openings, like the tongues of panting dogs

I swallowed drily

His?

Finn nodded, and beckoned me onwards

I stared at the boots and socks, aware of a new swirling somewhere inside my chest. Finn was telling the truth: there really was a stranger, a man, on the island

I kept following, but more slowly, allowing a distance to grow between us. What was it I was so afraid of? I didn't know exactly. The idea that there might be others – lands, people – out there, somewhere, had been an act of faith for so long that its sudden reality was overwhelming. I had imagined, if anything, a bottle floating to shore, inside it a message from a distant land. Or the tiny dot of a ship on the horizon, the day filled with its slow emergence from the heat haze. But the sudden presence, here and now, of a man on the island . . . it was too great a shock

In here, I heard Finn say. I looked up and saw his brown wiry body disappear into a stand of trees. I went to the spot where he had disappeared

Here you go, drink that. My sister's bringing food

I hesitated by the last tree, watching my brother's back as he squatted, the spine curved forward, his legs sprawled outward, like a frog's. His shadow was black on the dry yellow grass. I edged a little further round the tree, squinting to make out the shape of the stranger without being seen myself

Feel better? My sister was right behind me, I don't know what she's

He turned his neck and saw me, peering out, shy as a bird

Alice come on, what are you doing?

I felt my sweat-soaked face flush a deeper shade of red. Now I had no choice. I took a step forward, then another, and saw him

sunlight streaming over his naked torso

Hello Alice, I'm Will

Hast thou not dropped from heaven?

My tongue was lead; I could not speak. Instantly I hated him for transforming me into an idiot

What's that you've brought me?

Wordless, I placed the bags next to his body, which lay on the grass *hard shapes of his muscles moving under skin* and he sat up, watching me curiously. I looked away

Figs! Wonderful, I love the taste of figs

I stared at the trees. I hated my hair. I had never even thought about my hair until that moment

And. What's that, some kind of thin bread?

Pancakes said Finn

his eyes as the eyes of doves by the rivers of waters washed with milk his cheeks as a bed of spices as sweet-flowers his lips like lilies dropping sweet-smelling myrrh

No kidding, pancakes?

Try one, they're good

Finn turned to me and gasp-grinned He speaks the same language as we do!

Mmm, that's unbelievable, Finn. It tastes so good

Our Pa makes them

I felt light, dizzy, nauseous, as though I might faint at any moment. What the hell was wrong with me?

thou art beautiful my love as a sunrise comely as the dew on the grass terrible as an army with banners

Really? All on his own? That's amazing

They're only pancakes, I said, my voice a harsh croak, and the two of them stared at me. Chestnut-flour, milk and eggs. What's so amazing about that? I sounded like a nasty princess from one of the Tales

Well, Alice, I guess I'm so famished that any food seems pretty amazing to me *eyes like doves eyes cheeks like sweet flowers lips like lips like lips like lips like*

I hated him I hated him. I was such an ugly, frizzy-haired idiot. I would never ever speak to him again. I wanted him to vanish from the island. Our island. I wanted him to die from swimming in the poison sea. No, I wanted him never to have swum here, never to have contaminated us with his existence. I wanted the world to be nothing but still, toxic water, no humans left but the four of us. I wanted Pa's stories to be true

I might call him a thing divine for nothing natural I ever saw so noble a plague upon the tyrant that I serve I'll bear him no more sticks but follow thee thou wondrous man

Won't you sit down Alice? Have a pancake

I stare at the still-dark sky. Time passes so slowly. What lengthens Alice's hours? Not having that which, having, makes them short. Come day, come Will, thou night in day. Come gentle morning, come loving, golden dawn, give me my Will . . .

I go to the music room, where I sit, the pages open in a pool of candlelight, and read *Romeo and Juliet* again. The words take me to another land, another time, before the before. I am not here as I read, but in Verona, wherever that was, on a balcony, in a church, inside a dark crypt. Still, always, the story ends in death, in love thwarted and love eternal. I sigh, gravely. I should have read *The Tempest* instead. But my father is no Prospero, and I no sweet obedient Miranda. From the hall I hear him snoring through his door. He drank too much last night; he won't be up early today

You're still my little girl, you know

129

(Wine fumes and stubble, hairy hands grasping mine)

I know, Pa

And I'm still your Pa, aren't I?

(Yellowish eyes, greedy and pathetic, fireless now)

Of course

I love you Alice, please always remember that, no matter what I

(He's slurring his words but telling the truth)

It's OK, Pa, I love you too. And I know

(I'm pronouncing correctly but lying)

My little girl

I have done nothing but in care of thee, of thee, my dear one, thee, my daughter. O, a cherubin thou wast that did preserve me!

(How sharper than a serpent's tooth it is to have a thankless child.)

But soft! methinks I scent the morning air.

I will rise now, and go about the island, and in the fields and woods I will seek him whom my soul loveth.

I fetch a thick fleece from the bedroom and put it on. In the kitchen I take a bunch of grapes from the bowl, then move outside, closing the door behind me. The click of it shutting, and then silence. I put a grape in my mouth and crush it between my back teeth: the pip crunches, splinters, and the sweet juice flows over my tongue.

Yes, the sky is lightening now

XVIII

The silence is noisy as Hell. In the grey sultry midafternoon heat, birds and cicadas and bees and flies all twitter and pritter and buzz away; Goldie snores at the feet of his new master (who was it said dogs were loyal fuckers? They lie); and there's the clatter and clink of forks and knives on greasy plates, the gross symphony of chewing swallowing sniffing made by the four of us (me, Finn, Alice, HIM) at the table, and the awful deep harking of poor Daisy's cough, coming through the open window of her bedroom.

I eat some more flesh of The Deer That Will Killed. It is ASHES in my mouth. I drink more wine to help it down. God knows I hate the taste, the humiliation, but I need the strength it gives if I am ever to. Fuck it. I eat drink breathe hatred now, but it's no more than a drip-feed. It comes daily, in the same measure, and I need more and more of it merely to remain as I am. It will never give me the heart or muscle or the WILL to do what needs to be done. Vengeance is mine, saith the Lord, and I will repay. But the Lord was not feeble; he did not have a heart condition.

Hark hark hark. And then. Prayerrrrr. Spit in the bucket, her bubbling froth of phlegm streaked with blood. Poor Daisy. HE has contaminated her. She was never ill like this before. HE has damaged Finn's faith in me. HE has even stolen my dog from me. Man's best friend. Ever faithful companion. Fuck it.

As for Alice . . . O that my head were waters, and mine eyes a fountain of tears, that I might weep day and night for the fall of my beloved daughter! And yet, I am almost used to it now. I do not follow them any more. I do not watch over them, or seek to prevent their iniquities. I am blind. I turn a blind eye. But in my head and in my heart I am counting. Each kiss they steal is a blade in me that will equal a blade in HIM. Eye for eye, tooth for tooth, hand for hand, foot for foot, burning for burning, wound for wound, and the wages of sin is DEATH.

I am sick and tired of all this.

I am sick and I am tired.

I stand up. 'I'm going to check on Daisy.'

'Of course.' The viper's smile is polite, tolerant, respectful, generous, but I see the cunning and the malice and the venomous fangs beneath it. Get thee behind me, Satan. I walk into the ark, through the kitchen, and knock softly on Daisy's door.

Hark hark. 'Come.' Hark. 'In.'

I open the door, and there she is, my little girl, her face pale grey and shiny with sweat, golden hairs sticking to her forehead, kneeling in supplication before the reeking bucket.

'Hey Pa.' She hugs my knees as I stroke the crown of her head.

'Hey Daisy.' I kneel down next to her. 'How are you feeling?'

'A little better, I . . .' Hark hark hark. 'Better than I . . .' Hark hark hark. 'Well . . .' HARK. HARK. HARK. PRAYERRRRR.

I rub her back. She looks up at me out of one teary eye and murmurs, 'Say "There there" Pa.'

'There there, Daisy.' I rub her back some more. Then with the other hand, I stroke her hair back from her damp forehead and hold it in a pony tail as she coughs up more gunge into the bucket. Poor little Daisy. 'There there, honey.'

'It does work, doesn't it?' she says, when she's recovered from the last coughing fit. 'When you say "There there", I always feel better, don't I?'

'Of course.'

'It's really magic, isn't it Pa? Alice says words can't heal you, but they can, can't they?'

'They can if they're said with love.'

'I love you Pa,' she says suddenly, as though some great wave of emotion has forced the words from her mouth, and holds me tight around the chest.

'I love you too Daze. Very much.'

We stay like that for a while, until she says, 'I'm hungry.'

'Shall I make you some broth? That'd be good for you.'

She nods. 'I think I might go to bed for a while.'

'Feeling sleepy?'

'Uh-huh.'

She gets in bed and I lay the sheet over her chest, kiss her forehead – 'Good girl' – and go to the kitchen to make the broth. But HE and Finn are washing the dishes, there's no space, so I go outside and find Alice bent over the table, scrubbing it with a cloth. She's wearing Mary's white dress cut off at the *as is the mother so is the daughter therefore will I discover thy skirts upon thy face that thy shame may* Stop. I swallow and look away.

You have to tell her.

She doesn't listen.

You have to try.

I've tried, she never

You have to try AGAIN.

'Alice, can I talk to you?'

'Go ahead.' Still scrubbing. Her voice cold, neutral.

'Can we go somewhere more . . .?'

She stops scrubbing and looks up at me. 'Not again.'

'I need to talk to you. Let's go behind the ark. It's cooler there.'

She sighs. I take that as a yes, and walk round the ark, into shadow. A few seconds later, she follows. I sit with my back to the wooden wall, looking out at fields and sea, and pat the long grass next to me. Alice remains standing, her arms folded.

'What do you want to say?'

'You think you love him, don't you?'

'I do love him. I don't need to *think* about it at all.'

'He doesn't love you.'

'Yes he does.'

'How do you know?'

'I . . . know.'

'It's wishful thinking, Alice. You think he loves you because you think you love him and . . .'

'I *do* love him.'

'. . . and you want him to love you in the same way, but he *doesn't*, Alice. He doesn't. He's lying. He's using you.'

Her smile, cool and ironic, wobbles a little. 'And how would you know?'

'Because I know who . . .'

Tell her who he is.

I can't.

You must.

She must never

134

'Because I know what he is.'

'*What* he is? A man, you mean?'

'You're so young, Alice. You're not worldly wise. That's not your fault, of course, but you don't understand why people sometimes say and do things that aren't necessarily . . .'

She starts quoting Shakespeare at me, implying that I'm Prospero, and Will her Ferdinand. She's so clever, such a clever girl, but she's blind and deaf and doesn't even know it. I begin to grow angry.

'You're not listening to me, Alice.'

'Why should I listen to you tell me what I can and can't feel?'

'That's not what I'm . . .'

'Who I can and can't fall in love with?'

'Jesus fucking Christ. It's a teenage infatuation, Alice. We all go through them, we all grow out of them.'

'That's easy for you to say. You grew up surrounded by thousands of other people. I'm . . .'

'Yes yes, I know. But that's no reason to . . .'

'What do you think is going to happen to me? Who else will I ever meet, here on this island?'

Her words pierce me. 'Listen Alice, I understand it's not easy for you, but try to be reasonable . . .'

'But what you're saying isn't reasonable! If we're the only people left in the world . . .'

'I said maybe, I didn't say . . .'

'. . . then you'll die and we'll die and that will be the end. It makes no sense. If you think God saved us alone of all the human race, then how . . .'

Then how? Then how? I don't know I flash on Lot's daughters preserving their father's seed (they got him drunk it wasn't his fault how could it be a sin?) and look at Alice, I shudder, NO, and she reads my mind her face creases with disgust and

'I would rather die than do it with a filthy old man like you. Even if you weren't my father . . .'

The horizon turns red. Woe unto her that striveth with her maker! Shall the clay say to him that fashioneth it, What makest thou?

'Don't accuse me of . . .'

My fists clench.

'Go on,' she whispers, with teasing harlot eyes. 'Do it again.'

'Alice, don't make me lose my fucking temper.'

'Go on, hit me! Hit me! Go on, make me cry! That's all you . . .'

Tears are pouring from her eyes, suddenly, and I am unmanned. My little girl.

Sorry I'm so fucking sorry what do you want me to 'Alice.'

But she is gone. I follow her round the corner of the ark, and see her lost in HIS arms. He stares at me over her trembling shoulders.

You fucking touch my daughter and I'll fucking

'Why don't you go to bed?' His voice cold, superior, filled with contempt.

I have used thee, filth as thou art, with human care . . . till thou didst seek to violate the honour of my child.

Calm down, calm. I close my eyes

XIX

Yes, the sky is lightening now. I walk round the side of the ark and take the path that leads past the chicken shed *his face deformed by fury his two coarse hands covering the delicate neck*. A cockerel shrieks, and afterwards the silence seems to deepen. What can I hear? Some wind, perhaps; the faint shiver of leaves. I eat more grapes and keep walking. The air I breathe is dark grey, and so are all the objects around me: I can see where I'm going easily enough, but no colours emerge from the gloom. This is how the island was in my dream.

The heady smell of wine reaches my nostrils. I look over the vines stretching across to my right and remember the great barrels in the bamboo hut at the back of the ark. We picked and crushed the grapes three days ago. I love the taste of the new wine: it is still light and fizzy and has the same sweetness as these grapes. Only after the first moon does it begin to acquire that sourness, that heaviness which my father considers a sign of maturity. Animals are the same, and so are plants: in each living thing, youth is bliss and freshness, and all that follows weary decline. Oh let me stay young forever or let me.

I glance at the sky: there is still time. I walk back towards the hut. Inside, the air is cool and thick with fermentation. I climb the ladder of the nearest barrel, push aside the lid, and pull the string that dangles from its rim. The ladle emerges and I pour the dark grey liquid into my mouth. It *tastes* red. Another spoon, and another: a smile spreads across my face. Am I tipsy? Oh, what if I am! That which hath made him drunk hath made me bold, what hath quenched him hath given me fire.

I walk through the cornfield, the ranks of grey soldiers leaning over me, their coarse leaves brushing my face, and keep on until I reach the last line of apple trees. There, I turn and look backwards, but the ark is invisible behind the high curtain of maize. Feeling the tension drain from my body – they are all sleeping, they will not find me – I continue up the slope, over the hill, across the river. Ssssshhhhh . . . the water telling me to be quiet, not to make a sound.

I walk along the fence that divides the sheep from the goats. I am on the sheepside. I can see them, pale little clouds huddled in the far corner. Some of them start towards me, so I climb the fence, but the same thing happens with the goats. Wind and Rain come running, their meh-mehs so hopeful and excited that I do not have the heart to ignore them. I crouch down for a moment and stroke their warm flanks. This is all they want: caresses, love; they do not even meh for food. 'Rain, my Rain'

He came in while I was eating breakfast, while the others were out working

Phew, it's hot already out there. Nice and cool in here. Your father made this place, huh?

I didn't speak. I was too busy trying to eat the pancake without spilling blackberry jelly down my chin. I was blushing frantically at the thought of my hair, all frizzy from the night. Why did he have to come here so early? I hated him

Finn said this was your ark, that you all escaped the great flood inside it

His face was expressionless. I didn't know how to respond. Did he think Finn's story was childish nonsense, or did he believe it? How had *he* escaped the flood? I said nothing, drank my mint tea. I couldn't look him in the eyes

You know Alice, I don't think I've ever met anyone who disliked me so intensely as soon as they met me. Usually it takes a few days at least. A lopsided grin as he said this. What did I do to offend you?

Nothing I mumbled, standing up and taking my plate and cup to the sink

If you tell me what I did wrong, I might be able to put it right

You didn't do anything to offend me I replied. I washed the plate and cup, then put them on the draining board. I've got to go and work now

Listen, I know this is your island. Your family's, I mean. I know I came uninvited; that I'm an intruder, if you like. But

It's fine, I'm not offended. My voice had gone lighter, higher. I faked a smile. But I've got to go and work. He was blocking my way. My eyes were at the level of his shoulders, his throat. I trembled slightly. So if you'd let me pass

What work are you going to do? Maybe I could help

I've got to milk the goats first but

Oh will you show me how to milk the goats? Then maybe I wouldn't be quite so useless. I'd like to earn my keep at least. It seems wrong that you should keep sharing all your food and wine with me when I

All right, I'll show you

It wasn't worth arguing with him; he would only keep asking until I said yes. And anyway

We walked to the field where the goats were and I fetched the bucket and stool from their shelter. I placed the stool beside Rain, the bucket underneath, and stroked her back and head. She was the easiest. I didn't want to make myself look any more foolish in front of him. He knelt on the grass next to me, one hand resting on a leg of the stool. I could hardly breathe

Slowly the steady pulsing relaxed me. The hypnotic prrrddt-prrrddt of liquid hitting metal: the sound of morning, and solitude. Yes, solitude, that was it. I was on my own; there was no one else around. I closed my eyes, leaned my fore-head against Rain's flank, inhaled her goatish, earthy smell

Could I try?

I stood up and moved behind him. He smiled at me and sat on the stool

What's her name?

Rain

He stroked her flank. Don't worry Rain, I'm not going to hurt you. I may not be quite as smooth as Alice, but I'll do my best

You've done this before I said, accusing

Never. I swear

His hands, finer, smoother, gentler than my father's, squeezed and teased the last jets of milk from Rain

It took me ages to learn to do it that well

Maybe I had a better teacher than you?

I thought of Pa, frowning and muttering over my shoulder, and allowed a half-smile to show. No, I think you're just a natural. If you're telling the truth about never having done it before

He looked back over his shoulder. Why would I lie?

I shrugged. She's done

Oh. He stood up from the stool and stroked Rain affectionately on the back. Then he picked up the bucket as if it weighed nothing. As if it were empty. Where does the milk go, Alice?

In the big churn, behind the ark

He blinked in acknowledgement and walked away. I stood still, stroking Rain, watching his figure recede

'Oh Rain, you would miss him too, wouldn't you?' I nuzzle her, nose to nose, then, very firmly, I say goodbye and flee, knowing she will follow, but that she cannot pass through the boundary of her little world; that she must remain here, waiting for me, missing me. Is that how he will treat me? Is that all he feels for me?

I skip over the fence at the field's end, and walk up the next slope. I do not look back. Approaching the lake I

You said you'd take me

Oh not again Alice please it's so hot can't we just

You promised you'd take me and you broke your promise

I didn't promise. I said I

You promised. On my hundred and sixtieth moonday, you said

That's how you remember it

Pa don't lie to me, don't treat me like I'm Daisy

Stop shouting, Alice

Why, who's going to hear? I thought we were the only ones left in the world

Finn and Daisy get upset when you shout, you know they do

Damn Finn! Damn Daisy!

He looked at the ground. Through the trees I could hear my sister splashing in the shallow water of the lake. What exactly is it you want to know?

I don't know what I want to know, that's the whole point, isn't it? How can I know until I know?

like something has been stolen from my life and I can't even

You're not making much sense Alice

Lots of things don't make sense here

Like what? Maybe I can explain

Like the sea, I said. Quietly. Triumphantly. I had been thinking about the sea for a long, long time

A telltale pause, then an inhalation of breath

What about it?

Well in Shakespeare the sea's always moving. There are waves and tides and tempests and

And our sea is so calm and still?

Yes, and in Shakespeare it has a special smell, it makes a special sound

I know, Alice, I remember it well. It smelled of salt and iron, and it made a sort of gigantic shushing noise, like a thousand rivers in chorus. The waves came in and went away, all the time. It was beautiful, the sea

My father's eyes had a kind of rapture in them

So why isn't ours like that?

It's because of the flood, Alice. The sea's never been the same since the flood

For a second I didn't know what to say

Is that what you've been getting so

Pa (a far-off voice). Pa, what's Daisy doing?

He sighed and stood up

Damn Daisy, I said, I want to

He screamed, and ran towards his drowning daughter

I walk round the lake until I reach the edge of the forest. I find our pine tree, the one we engraved. It was here that he told me to meet him. *I will, Will, I will.* At dawn, he said. The air here is dark but when I look up at the sky I can see it has grown lighter.

Will isn't here.

I sought him, but I found him not.

Thus have I had thee as a dream doth flatter: in sleep a queen, but waking no such matter. Is he truly gone, then? What, will I never see him again?

You don't know what he is Alice I know you love him but you shouldn't put so much he's not to be trusted he's not what he says he is I fear you're going be hurt if you

I close my eyes then look once again at the horizon. It really isn't dawn yet. Still there is not a single colour in the landscape, and that brightness has barely begun to spread. I am early; that's why he isn't here. I have only to wait.

To wait, to wait, to woo.

O my dove, that art in the shadows of the forest, in the secret places of the shore, let me see thy countenance, let me hear thy voice.

Where could he be? I walk through the long grass by the edge of the woods and down the slope towards my field. Yes, I will wait there and dream of him; the edge of the forest will be visible from there. *No not here, come, I know a better place*

Their faces are all turned away from me. They, like me, are watching the eastern horizon, waiting for their master to come and cover them with glory. Their heads still droop at this hour, as if they are sad. I touch the slender stalk of one near me. He is smaller than his fellows; he comes up only to my thigh. I stroke the petals from behind and, crouching, turn his face to mine. Trace the invisible spirals with my fingertips, breathe in the sweet delicate scent and put the face to my lips. Sunflower kiss. I pluck a petal from the outer ring and whisper

'He loves me.'

I drop the petal to the ground and pull another.

'He loves me not.'

A game my mother taught me. The memory flickers for the briefest moment in my mind, is whole, and then dissolves, so that no amount of wanting will restore it. I sigh. Did she truly teach me this? Well, who else could have done? But here . . . was it *here*? Soon, Alice. You'll know soon. If.

'He loves me'

Alice can we go somewhere quiet, somewhere we can be alone?

Of course, do you

In here? The corn's grown so tall, nobody will see us

No not here. Come, I know a better place

The sunflowers, I never thought

You have to crawl down here, but they grow taller in the middle, you'll see. I come here all the time to be alone. Used to

These flowers are incredible. They're just huge how did your father

They're not his, they're mine. I ploughed the ground and I planted the seeds and I water the soil. He makes the oil afterwards, but the flowers are mine. The field is mine

They're beautiful Alice

I love them too, especially when they're young and they

still turn their heads to the sun. The way they follow it across the sky. When they get older the stems go hard and they just look east all day

I never knew that

his face close to mine, our breaths merging, in the shadows, amid sunflowers, in the shadows of their stalks and

I read a story when I was young, about a girl called Clytie, who fell in love with the god of the sun, his name was Apollo, and all she'd do, all day, day after day, was watch his golden chariot move through the heavens

his eyes, the pupils huge, the air cool and scented, amid sunflowers, in the shadows, his fingers brushed linen and I

From east to west, day after day, watching it cross the sky, until after nine days she was turned into a sunflower

He laughs, looks puzzled

I guess there are worse things you could turn into

Yes. In my next life I'd like to be a sunflower. Only I wouldn't want to grow old. Someone would have to pick me, kill me, before my stem grew hard and I couldn't turn my face any more

his lips opened slightly showing teeth then closed again the sound of his

I'd like to be a bird one day too, one of the small birds, I love the way they dart between trees. I don't think I could ever be sad if I had wings. Loneliness would just evaporate as you flew, don't you think?

breath and my own the feel of my pulse in my throat my tongue on my lips his

Then again, the way they call to each other every morning and evening, they must sometimes feel alone. Would a bird still sing if it were the last bird on earth? That would be a sad sound. Even wings might not erase that sadness

Alice, the way you talk sometimes it's

lips, O you the doors of breath

It's what?

I don't know, like a poem or something. I've never heard anyone talk like that before

his fingers brushed linen and his lips opened the doors of breath our faces moving closer slowly so slowly

I wanted to ask about before, about beyond, about the other people he had heard speak, about how they sounded, why they were different, was there something wrong with me, but I dared not break the spell. I kept silent, made my lips like his, felt myself slide forward, the two of us drawn together inexorably, like slow magnets

O! a kiss. Stop his mouth with a kiss. Let him kiss me with the kisses of his mouth. Then come kiss me

amid sunflowers, in the shadows of their stalks and heads, my lips touched his and

Thy lips, O my love, drop as the honeycomb: honey and milk are under thy tongue

and his lips touched lips touched lips touched lips and I

'He loves me.'

The final petal falls to the ground

XX

Calm down, calm. I close my eyes.

When I open them again, the fornicators have disappeared. Gone to the lake, I guess, or. No. I don't want to know. Don't want to think about it.

I go into the kitchen and find Finn, gaunt-faced, sitting at the table alone, staring into thin air.

'You want to help me make some broth for Daisy?'

He looks up, then shakes his head wearily. 'I'm going for a walk.'

'Finn, you're not going to follow them again, are you?'

'No.' He squints at me, miserable and defensive.

'It doesn't help anyone when you spy on them, you know. It only . . .'

'I said I'm NOT going to follow them.' Hostile now, he stalks off. Finn has changed this summer. Is changing. He has gone into darkness, just as I knew he would, and the darkness has gone into him.

I make a broth for Daisy, clean the kitchen while I let it cool, then spoonfeed it to her in bed. Afterwards she smiles at me, then falls asleep. I stand there, stroking her hair, for what feels like hours. I am a good father, yes I am. And Daisy still loves and trusts me, even if no one else.

I go back to the kitchen and pour some wine, take it outside and sit under the branch roof, watching the trees move slightly in the wind. I imagine the fornicators in the sunflowers and sadness engulfs me. My face is foul with weeping, and on my eyelids is the shadow of death. After two more glasses of wine, weariness creeps over me and I go to bed. Is death like sleep, I wonder.

I have bad dreams. HORRIBLE dreams.

When I wake up, the insides of my head are all twisted up like my sheets. I walk blearily through the corridor and into the kitchen, where I find Daisy sitting with the bucket between her legs, coughing, shivering, her face glazed with sweat. I touch her forehead: it's hot again.

'You should be in bed, angel. What are you doing out here?'

She looks at me with dull eyes. 'They wanted the room. I said you'd told me to stay in bed, but they said I could go to sleep in your bed if I was tired. But I went in your room and you were lying across all the bed so I came here instead.'

There is no bitterness in her voice, only a sort of tired whine.

I ask the question, even though I already know the answer. 'Daisy, who wanted the room?'

'Will and Alice.'

The kitchen wall is red.

'I'll be back in a while, Daisy.'

I touch her shoulder, then walk to the bedroom door. Knock three times. Hear a breath-held silence. Try the handle. The door's blocked somehow. BANG BANG BANG the door with the flat of my palm. The door is red.

'Just a minute.' Will's voice behind the door. He sounds bored, irritated.

My hands are red as they slam against the door again. 'OPEN THE FUCKING DOOR!'

'Just a *minute*.'

I take two steps back and ram my shoulder against the door. It gives a few inches and I look through the gap at the corner of the red bunk, the red floor, the red wall. My shoulder aches but I don't fucking care I smash it into the door again, then push push push. He's shoved the dresser against it the fucking I push and push until the gap is wide enough for my body to slip through. My shoulder is screaming with fucking pain. The fornicators stare at me through the bloodcoloured air. WHAT IS THIS THAT THOU HAST DONE? There's silence except for somewhere the sound of Daisy coughing and crying. I stare at the fornicators. Are they embarrassed or angry? I can't tell and I don't fucking care. I yell in their faces, all the hatred and fury in my heart. I yell my fury that they kicked poor sick Daisy out of her bed so they could satisfy their endless foul lusts and why? Fucking why? I do not stop them kissing and laughing and rolling around naked in the dirt of the fucking sunflowers. I do not ban them from defiling the lake or the trees that encircle it. I turn a blind eye. I swallow my bile. So why why WHY must they come here, to the ark I built with my own hands, for the shelter of my family, and despoil it with their grimy panting filthy fucking urges the fucking whores? I kick the red beds punch the red walls as I rage and HE stands in front of her, like some kind of protector, but *I* am the protector you fucking son of a bitch. And she, SHE deserves whatever I yell at her whatever I do to her (I'm not sorry I'm not fucking sorry what the hell reason) and if thou say in thy heart, Wherefore come these things upon me? For the greatness of thine iniquity are thy skirts discovered and thy heels made bare. Because thou hast forgotten me, Alice, and trusted in falsehood. I have seen thine adulteries, and thy neighings, the lewdness of thy whoredom, and thine abominations on the hills and in the fields, by the lake and in the sunflowers. Woe unto thee, Alice! Wilt thou not . . .

The wasps! I hold my chest, close my eyes, breathe slowly, until the blood drains from my vision and the hammering of my heart is no longer as loud as my palms banging on the door. Calm down, calm. Until the swarm inside me ceases its stinging buzz. Calm.

I open my eyes.

Their four eyes are cold and seething. Hatred pours from them, like pale fire. I feel weak, drained, empty.

HE speaks, his throat tight with anger. 'I want to talk to you alone. There is a conversation we need to have.' His words vibrate. 'Did you hear me? We need to talk.'

'Later,' I say, suddenly weary. 'This evening, when the children are in bed.'

He nods. 'All right. But you ARE going to listen to me.'

'Get out of this room now. Daisy needs to lie down in bed.'

They look at me in astonishment, but I push past them. Then I see Daisy, standing in the gap between the door and the doorframe, her face streaked with water.

'Daze?'

Her lips wobble and she runs away.

I go into the corridor.

'Daisy? It's all right. I was only angry at them for.' Sorry I'm so sorry what can I. 'Daisy, come and see Pa. Listen to me.'

I find her in the music room, curled in a ball on my chair. She is shivering and sobbing, but very quietly, as though she doesn't want to be heard.

'Daisy, I'm sorry. I lost my temper, that's all.' I stroke her trembling shoulder. 'There there, Daisy. Everything's going to be all right. This is like the part of the fairy tale where everything goes bad. But the happy ending is coming soon. You know it is, don't you?'

I am bending down close to her, whispering in her ear. She looks up at me, with hope (fear?) in her eyes, and then flings her arms round my neck.

'I was scared,' she blurts, sobbing.

'I'm sorry, Daisy, I'm so sorry I scared you. But it's all right now. Everything's all right now. There there, there there.'

I tidy up the mess in her bedroom

XXI

The final petal falls to the ground. He loves me. He will come. I look up at the sky, which is milk-grey now, like snow on a moonless night, then I turn to the west, to the edge of the forest.

All is grey, empty, silent.

I sought him, but I found him not.

I call his name, softly, my voice rising as I speak so it sounds like a question.

Will? Will? Will?

Won't. Shan't. Can't.

Before I am even aware of having made a decision, my legs are striding along the edge of the woods. I watch my feet in the long grass as I walk: there are traps here, hidden, metal mouths waiting to spring shut. Now I hear the birds' dawn chorus. When did they start singing? I move more quickly, away from the trees and the long grass, down the slope, towards the shore.

I take the last path through the forest and follow its gentle curve. The shortcut. My brother and my father do not know about this path. Its entrance is concealed. It is ours. How many times have I walked its narrow, pine-scented length, almost floating with the joy of anticipation? Once, early on in the summer, a couple of days after that first kiss in the sunflowers, before the spy and the tyrant discovered us, I bumped into him here. No, not there, *here*, yes, just past that boulder

Alice, I
Hello Will
I was just coming to see you
I was coming to see *you*
We laughed at the same time. I could feel his eyes moving over my legs and shoulders, which were bare, and my lips, which were scarlet and glistening from the berry juice I'd rubbed on them
Hot day
It's cool in here though
in the shadows
That's true. Do you want to
Yes
I mean, shall we
Yes, Will
You look different today
I feel different
Oh. What if your father
He's asleep. He won't wake up till evening
So you
Yes Will yes yes yes
The path leads to a scrubby clearing, from where you can see a small patch of sea. There is a kind of luminescence on its surface. Can that really be the sun? I look to the east, but my view is blocked by dark pine trees. The spy and the tyrant might be stirring now. I need to hurry. I cross the clearing and enter the stand of trees. I call his name.

Silence.

Make haste, my beloved!

I call again, then push open the door of his shelter. The familiar smell of him. It's dark inside so I crouch down and crawl across the earth floor, my hands stroking, touching, expecting to feel, at any moment, the silky soft skin of his sleeping bag . . .

There is nothing here but cold earth. His clothes have gone, his boots, his rucksack. There is nothing left.

I have sworn thee fair and thought thee bright who art as black as hell, as dark as night.

There is a terrible chasm gaping in my chest. Fear, Fear, and at its heels, like a tiny persistent dog, hope. Is it possible I have missed him? What if he went the other way while I took the path in the woods? But why would he climb over rocks on the beach, carrying all his belongings, when there was an easier, quicker way? Unless there were another shortcut. A secret. A secret even from me. Or what if he were already inside the forest? What if he were in there, even when I arrived, doing something, something important, and only came out at dawn, expecting to see me, and I were.

I have been so stupid. Such an idiot.

I emerge from the shelter and run back the way I came. Above the clearing the sky is pale blue, the pine needles all shine green. I am too late, the sun has risen, he is. Don't think Alice, only run. *Run along the path that he run past the boulder where I run out of the forest and along by the sunflowers where we*

I slow down as I reach the edge of the wood and stare at our lonely pine tree. The birdsong like a thousand knives being sharpened. The leaves on the trees so green they hurt my eyes. I am panting, my heart in my neck.

He isn't here. He isn't coming.

I sought him, but I could not find him; I called him, but he gave no answer.

I feel

I feel like there is a hole in my soul.

'I was wondering where you'd got to.'

I turn and stare. He smiles. Am I dreaming? But no, there he is: true, solid, palpable. Will. Not gone. Will oh Will oh Will. I hold him so tight he gasps, then laughs. I kiss his lips, where they're swollen and split. I kiss his neck, where it's bruised. His eyes are as the eyes of doves, but one of them is black. I found him whom my soul loveth: I held him and would not let him go.

I am shaking all over.

'I went to your shelter I thought you were.'

'I was inside the woods, hiding my things.'

I remember the bare earth floor. 'Why, you're not leaving?'

'All will be revealed Alice. Come on, there's no time to lose.'

'Where are we going?'

'We can talk in the forest. Let's go.'

Tell me you're not leaving promise me you won't ever swear it or I'll

But I do not speak a word.

We walk, the two of us, side by side. Some days, when we're alone and can't be seen, he holds my hand while we walk, but today he doesn't. He is brisker than normal, almost like another person. I want to ask him where we're going, but there is something forbidding about his face this morning. And besides, I am still floating on a cloud of my own relief. He hasn't gone. He is here with me. The bad dream hasn't come true. Not yet.

Inside the forest it is as cool and dim as if the sun had not yet risen. I fall into a kind of trance, listening to the rustle and flap my trainers make as they hit the ground, tuning in and out of the birdsong, which grows more scattered the deeper in we go. Not knives now, but wood nymphs' laughter. The path narrows, twists, sometimes disappears.

I am following Will, though he has, as far as I know, been here only twice. I have been here three times. The first time I was alone, and frightened. The second time, I took Will to see my father's wooden cabin, but it was locked. The last time, three days ago, he took me

Bending down, touching the black windows in the ground. Talking to himself, like I was no longer there

What are they?

They're solar panels, Alice. They make electricity

He unlocked the door with a key and we entered. Will pointed at one of the white boxes on the desk

You know what this is Alice?

I shook my head.

It's called a computer

A computer. As I said the word, the memory flickered within me. Pa had told us about them, once before. Last winter, I think, during those long dark snowbound days. What was it he had said? Special machines with the whole world inside them. Ask them a question and they'd tell you the answer. But people grew addicted to them, that's what he said. They were dangerous because they were addictive. Once you started looking into the screen, you couldn't pull yourself away. People spent their lives inside computers and forgot the real world in which they lived. And yet my father had one. Here. And never told us

Contaminated

Will touched another of the boxes. And this?

I shook my head

A printer. And these?

I don't know what anything is

He touched my shoulder. Don't worry Alice, you will. He stared away from me for a moment, then walked over to the books that lined the walls. Quite a reader your father. He pulled out a few books and flicked through them, said some of the titles out loud, laughed gently under his breath

What's funny?

Nothing. Really, it's nothing. What's behind that door?

I don't know

Will tried a few keys before he found the one that fitted

Will, where did you get those?

I stole them. He grinned at me

But what if he

Alice, I used to be frightened of your father. But I'm not any more. I'm stronger than him now

Yes, I know you are. But he has guns, knives

Not any more he doesn't

Oh

We went through to the next room. It was full of boxes. Hundreds of them

Are these computers too?

No, he smiled. No. These are just boxes. The question is

He walked over and picked one up

What's inside them

A ripping sound and the top of the box opened out in two halves. Will looked inside

What is it?

See for yourself

I moved over to him and peered inside. There was a pair of trainers, just like the ones I was wearing, only these were white, unstained, and slightly bigger

He opened another box and another and another. Large boxes and small boxes, round boxes and rectangular boxes. Shirts, skirts, jeans, bikinis, boots, hats, underwear spilled over the floor, all bright and clean. A strange smell in the air. Quietly he said Enough clothes to last a lifetime

We walk in the direction of the house. It is still quite dark. I watch as Will unlocks the door, then follow him inside and stare through the gloom. 'Have you got a candle?' I ask.

He touches the wall and there's a sound like an army of metal butterflies in flight, then a sudden blaze of whiteness, as if a hundred candles had all been lit at once.

'Don't worry, Alice, it's just an electric light. You don't remember these?'

I shake my head, blinking in the dazzle

XXII

I tidy up the mess in her bedroom and put Daisy back to bed. There is no sign of Alice or HIM. I cross Finn coming into the ark as I go out.

'Where are you going?' he asks.

'Nowhere. I've got something to do. I'll be back soon.'

We look at each other.

'Where did you go?' I ask.

'Nowhere.'

O Finn.

But I do not have time to deal with this now. I walk quickly through the gardens and up through the orchard. The sky is darkening, not with the onset of night, but with that bluish bruising that presages a storm. The wind whips my face as I mount the plateau. On I go until I reach the Afterwoods, and from there follow the path to the cabin. Between the solars, to the door. I slide the key into the lock, but the door opens without me turning the key. I frown, walk inside. Did I forget to lock the door last time I was here?

I switch on the lights. Tinny humming. I squint through the neon glare. There, on the desk – not locked in the drawer, as it should be – is my journal. I stare at its black cover and feel like I am staring into a bottomless abyss. No. *They must never.* I take my lighter from the drawer, flick its sparkwheel and touch the blue flame to the edge of the journal's pages. My words are eaten up, the past consumed. The smoke makes me cough, it brings tears to my eyes. I hold on to the book's cover until the heat becomes unbearable, then I let go. It drops to the floor and I stamp out the fire. Black ash stains the boards beneath my boots.

Gone, all gone. A lifetime ago, a world away.

In case of my death or disappearance . . . but it is too late for that now. My hope is dying, my dreams disappearing. I must act to save them, even if it means . . .

Whatever it means.

I walk to the back room, but that door too is unlocked. Inside, boxes have been torn open and there are clothes strewn all over the floor. The wasps murmur inside me. Calm, stay calm. I walk to the cabinet.

The shotgun has gone. The pistol has gone. And so has all the ammunition.

I am going to fucking kill you fucking.

Eye for eye tooth for tooth burning for burning wound for wound blade for blade.

Calm down, calm.

HE has been here. I look around. What has he seen? What does he know? What does SHE know?

Fear and fury, like two halves of a fiery wheel rolling inside my mind, each flashing up their side in turn. Fear. Fury. Fear. Fury.

FEAR.

FURY.

FEAR.

I walk back to the ark, talking to myself to soothe the wasps' buzzing. I need to remain cool, calm, composed.

There is a conversation we need to have.

It is coming. That which is crooked cannot be made straight and that which is coming cannot be stopped.

O let me do evil, that good may come.

For the thing which I greatly feared is come upon me, and that which I was afraid of is come unto me.

To every thing there is a season. A time to be born, and a time to die. A time to plant, and a time to RIP UP that which is planted from the ground. A time to love and a time to hate, a time to build up and a time to SMASH DOWN into tiny pieces. A time to kill and a time to kill and a time to FUCKING KILL YOU YOU FUCKING.

Calm, calm down. Listen to him first, it may not be what you think. It may not be what you fear.

Fury.

Fear.

Fury.

Fear.

Back in the ark, I fix supper

XXIII

I shake my head, blinking in the dazzle.

'Well well well,' says Will, and I look to where he's looking. On the floor by Pa's desk is a book, its cover spread open, and a heap of black ashes.

'What is all this?'

'Something your father didn't want you to read, apparently.'

I bend down and pick up the book. On the front page, written in the cramped, jagged handwriting that I recognise as my father's, are these words:

IN CASE OF MY DEATH OR DISAPPEARANCE
What you are reading now you should <u>only</u> be reading if I have died or vanished from the island. Leave it a day or so, children, but no longer than that. If I'm not back after two days, then something is wrong. I would never leave you that long.

(Do <u>not</u> read this book if am still here or I will be very very angry.)

I look up at Will. 'You know what this is?'

He nods. 'Your father's journal. It's a shame he burned it. I should have taken it earlier, when I had the chance.'

He walks behind me and looks over my shoulder. 'I think there's still enough for you to get the idea. Do you want to read some now?'

'Do we have time? I thought you were in a rush.'

'There's something I've got to do here, so you may as well read while you wait. I'll tell you when it's time to go.'

Nervously, I sit in my father's chair and read the first, half-burnt page.

There was an earthquake yesterday. It was only minor – 5.5 on the Richter scale – but since then I just don't seem to see anything the same way. It's like I'm looking through new eyes, like what I saw before was a movie screen and it's suddenly been ripped away and only NOW am I seeing what was behind it, all that time. I look out the window at the pool, the electric fence, the ocean, and I can't shake the feeling that there's something unreal about it all, something prideful and doomed, like this is the Tower of Babel and soon it'll come crashing down. I look at the clothes in our wardrobe, I look at the faces around the table at meetings in work, and I just want to laugh. Or vomit. Or scream. It's crazy, nothing seems to matter or make sense any more. Nothing but Mary and Alice. Mary keeps telling me to lie down or take a holiday or a happy pill but she doesn't understand, this is . . .

Below that, the paper is ragged and blackened, the words unreadable. I stare at the words I've just read, pulse racing. My *father* wrote this? I skip a few pages and read on.

. . . most humiliating night of my life. The maid let me in and showed me through to Christian's office. I entered and he was sat behind the desk, pretending not to have heard me, his face all serious and concentrated. Just because he wanted to make me clear my throat, the prick. Then he looked up and smiled and said 'Ah, Ben,' in that phony, manly, all-friends-together voice of his. Two hours later he finally offered me (with the most incredible condescension) a job digging swimming pools for a company called Deep Blue Heaven which is run by an old college buddy of his. I think he was pretty surprised when I accepted. He thought I'd blanch as soon as I heard the salary etc, but as much as I hate and mistrust that bastard, I have to say this job sounds perfect. Physical, outdoors, stress-free, and I'm home by six every day. Of course we'll have to tighten the . . .

I don't know who Christian is, so I keep flicking through the pages, scanning for that magic name, those four letters which signify my mother: M-a-r-y.

. . . heard another child from the neighborhood got kidnapped today. The same Sins Of The Fathers group suspected. Mary says she knows the family. That's seven now, and the video of the last one being crucified is on the fucking net. Mary keeps repeating what Christian says about it, that the ringleaders should be executed on live TV blah blah but she doesn't see that killing these maniacs will change nothing, that the real culprit is all around us – in all the bullshit pouring from the moving mouths on TV, in the Coke and Sprite we drink and the Nike and Gap we wear, in the Stars and Stripes that hangs from the wall of Alice's preschool and the pledge of allegiance they make her recite every morning. Mary says I'm so full of hate she hardly knows me, but I don't WANT to be like this. I hate the President for MAKING ME HATE. I'm angry at being made so goddamn angry. I just want to forget this world and love my kids, bring them up somewhere they won't be 'white Americans', where they won't be tainted by . . .

. . . sad and frustrated at not being allowed to even say hello to them, and it was so fucking hot and I felt suddenly sick of digging pools, sick of everything, so I quit on the spot and didn't say goodbye, just got in my car and drove. Left the city behind. Went east and north. Slept by Mono Lake. The next morning was beautiful but there were tourists fucking everywhere so I got back in the car and kept driving, turning off major roads whenever I could and following smaller mountain tracks. So many times, this led me nowhere and I had to turn back, but late afternoon on the third day I found a track that passed between two hills and entered the widest, most gloriously empty valley. Not a single habitation or vehicle or human being anywhere to be seen, only forests and lakes and meadows, wild goats and circling hawks . . . and, at the far end of the valley, lonely and magnificent, this mountain. Soon as I got here, I knew it. Everything crystallised. This is the place. This is . . .

. . . I'm learning to almost enjoy the lying. I do it so often now that I have forgotten how it feels to be honest. In some ways this depresses me, in other ways it elates me.

Lying is wrong. I do believe that, with all my heart. But, at this (crucial) moment in time, lying is the only way to achieve what I know to be right. So I do it, and I do it well. My conscience is clear.

Lying to Christian in order to make him help me find this job was sheer pleasure, the subtlest kind of revenge. Lying at work is easy but unchallenging; no one in the agency would ever guess that I was laughing at them behind my furrowed brow and pursed lips.

But lying to Mary is harder, and I feel bad about it. One day soon I will tell her, but not now. She wouldn't understand. As it is, she suspects me of deceiving her. But she thinks I'm having an affair. Ha! Maybe when she finds out the truth she'll be relieved rather than horrified? . . .

. . .
mini-digger
trailer
cement mixer
circular saw/chainsaw/hacksaws & bowsaws
spades/forks/hammers etc
readymix cement × 100 bags
wooden planking (600m?)
electrical wiring (ask JP)
guttering/roof tiles/foil insulation/tarpaulin/plastic sheeting
woodburner & kitchen range
sand/gravel/pebbles
candles/matches/lighters + fuel
liners/pumps/filters
. . .

. . . thank You Lord, thank you President Mercer, this war is exactly what I've been praying for. I never thought I would write that, but on top of all the other disasters of the past six months it was enough to tip Mary over the edge. She cried on my shoulder, watching the news tonight. We could hear Daisy breathing through the baby monitor and M said 'What kind of world have we brought our children into?'

She sobbed. I comforted her, hugged and kissed her, then asked how she would feel about moving away from the city. Moving to a place where the war would never reach us. A place far away from all the earth's troubles.

'Oh God, if only we could,' she said.

'What if I told you that we can do exactly that, Mary?'

She stared at me then. I had her attention.

'You think I've been deceiving you, don't you?'

'I . . . what? No, it's just that . . .'

'You were right. I *have* been deceiving you Mary. But not in the . . .

. . . It's 1.30am as I write this, and in two hours we will leave. The dead of night. I've written the note to Christian, telling him we're going to Mexico and not to follow us, and Mary's copied it out and posted it. She was reluctant to do this as she hates dishonesty, but I persuaded her it was necessary. She does whatever I tell her nowadays. Fear makes a person more malleable. All she cares about is the safety of the children.

For the last few days she's been twitchy, desperate to go, but personally I've enjoyed saying goodbye to LA. Going through the motions at work, counting down the hours, knowing everything was ready and in place. Savouring those small miseries of city life – freeway jams, toxic smogs, junk food – sweetened by the knowledge that I was about to leave it all behind, that this would be my last styrofoam cup of bad coffee, my final breath of gasoline-tainted air. I've never felt calmer or happier in my life.

Looks like the rain's stopped now . . .

A touch on my shoulder and the details of the present reassemble themselves around me. Inside my father's cabin.

Will's voice saying, 'Time to go, Alice. Don't worry, you can read the rest later.'

Obediently I pass the book to Will. He drops it into the rucksack, and we go outside. The tyrant's strange words are circling my mind, like half-glimpsed memories, or faces seen in dreams.

Looks like the rain's stopped now

I don't know what to think, how to feel.

We walk until we reach a fork in the path. Will, unhesitating, goes right. I follow. I am now deeper inside the forest than I have ever been in my life. I begin to guess where we must be headed.

Something flickers in the corner of my eye

XXIV

Back in the ark, I fix supper and then check on Daisy. I change her sheets and pillow, which are soaked, but her forehead feels much cooler and her eyes are brighter. Finn is more relaxed too, or at least not so miserable. I guess he's been talking to Snowy. The other two keep out of my way.

In the evening we all eat together, outside. No one mentions what happened this afternoon. We talk about the sky, which is blue-black in the west, and the air, which feels thick and charged. Another storm is coming. As we tidy away the empty plates, sheet lightning illuminates the whole island. The Afterwoods rear up in brief flashing silhouette, then vanish into darkness again.

The wheel in my mind has stopped rolling. It's stuck on Fear.

I drink more wine. It numbs the pain, it dulls the dread. A little.

I kiss Finn and Daisy goodnight, then Alice follows them into the bedroom. She looks as nervous as I feel.

I turn to Will. 'Come on then. Let's go through to the music room.'

And face the music.

I offer him wine, but he refuses so I pour myself a big one and drink it as I listen. As I listen to him talk.

The excuses. The preliminaries. The throat-clearing. The due respect paid to my position as blah blah blah.

Get to the fucking point you fucking. Drink more wine it calms the wasps it numbs their stings. His face fades in and out of focus I'm falling asleep here get to the.

'OK. This is my point. Alice deserves to know. If you do not tell her tomorrow, I'll tell her myself. I just thought it'd be fair to warn you in advance, to give you the chance to . . .'

'Deserves to know WHAT? Tell her WHAT?'

'About her mother.'

They must never never

'WHAT about her mother?'

'She deserves to know her mother is alive.'

'Keep your voice down you fucking.'

'What? I'm not the one who's shouting.'

'Her mother is dead.'

'You know perfectly well that's not

Her mother is dead she drowned beneath the waves saving baby Daisy when in the storm the great flood when we were in the ark I was inside with Finn and Mary Mary (quite contrary) was out on the deck with Daze in her arms because she wanted to get some fresh air and but the wind was blowing strong still and the waves were crashing high and and I guess she musta let Daisy slip somehow and O God I can imagine how she musta felt like how I felt when I saw her golden hair on the lake's surface and thought O my daughter Daisy O my daughter and but she was brave Mary yes she was she proved it then she dived in into the sea and swam down and somehow musta grasped hold of Daisy and pushed her up up above the surface so she could breathe again and I I was on deck by now because I'd heard her screams and I saw my baby lifted up above the waves and I tied myself with rope to

169

the ark because no I wasn't a coward Father no I wasn't I was thinking clearly not panicking because I knew the sea was so strong filled with the wrath of the Lord and if I drowned who would look after Finn and Alice who would watch over them they would be and I tied myself to the ark and dived into the sea and took Daisy from Mary's hands and clambered on deck and slapped her back and seawater came pouring out her mouth and she screamed and I knew (O God the relief) she was alive ALIVE and don't interrupt me you fuck and I I I searched the waves for my wife for Mary but I couldn't see her anywhere and no I didn't give up I am not a coward I jumped off the ark making sure the rope was fast and dived down as far as I could into the water and looked for her but she wasn't there wasn't anywhere and I knew she musta stop interrupting me I'm talking here you fucking and I knew she musta just let go that she was too weak to keep swimming against that great tide but she knew she'd saved her child and that was enough and she'd just let herself go beneath the waves and we all love and remember her she will always be their mother but she is DEAD.

He stares at me open-mouthed. 'You can't believe that, can you? You can't believe your own lies.'

'*I* am not the liar here!'

'Aunt Mary is not dead. She's alive and well and living in.'

'Keep your fucking voice down.'

'I'm talking normally. You're the one who's shouting.'

I move my face close to his and hiss: 'You are not going to tell my daughter those lies.'

He pulls his face away. 'Your breath stinks. You're drunk.'

Hissing in his ear: 'You tell Alice those lies and I'll fucking kill you you fucking.'

'Surely you don't really.'

'Mary is dead and you will be too if you.'

'She's alive. Who do you think sent me here to.'

'What the HELL gives you the right to come here and spread your lies your poison your contamination you fucking.'

'I think what you've done is morally wrong and Alice deserves to.'

'How the fuck can you DARE YOU talk to me about morals when your own fucking father was.'

'You're going to wake up the children, you know. Is that what you want? You want them to find out the truth like this? I really think you should calm down now, so we can.'

I'm not going to fucking calm down you patronising snotnosed son of a fucking bitch you come here bringing lies and poison and contamination and you worm your way into my trust by lying and lying and then you have the nerve the gall to strip to seduce my daughter to take advantage of her vulnerabilty and I have used thee filth as thou art with human care till thou didst seek to violate and you break into my private cabin that belongs to ME and you steal my fucking guns you fuck and now and now you come here and talk to me about morals and you want to lie to my daughter to fill her head and heart with false hopes dreams delusions yes that's what they are and you want to take her away from me back to your foul and bloody Babylon well I will never let that happen do you understand me I thought you understood me the first time but O no thou hast fenced up my way that I cannot pass and thou hast set darkness in my paths thou hast stripped me of my glory and taken my daughter from my side thou hast destroyed me but NO I will destroy you instead you fucking eye for eye tooth for tooth hand for hand burning for burning wound for wound blade for blade and the wages of sin is.

He's up against the wall, in the corner of the music room, his O so handsome young face turned grey as a cloud, his eyes no longer smiling but half-popped out with terror. The words keep pouring out my mouth

XXV

Something flickers in the corner of my eye. I squint. And between trees I see it, running through the woods. A deer

Will and Finn carried it back between them, that poor sweet beautiful beast. They heaved it to the floor of the kitchen, on top of the old bloodstained sheet, and began slicing it open. I couldn't watch. But they were so happy with their kill, so proud

Will made the venison stew that evening. It cooked all night on the range. I sweated in my dreams

We ate it the next day, at lunch. The day before yesterday. Daisy was in her room; we could hear her coughing. I played footsie with Will under the table. Footsie: he taught me that word. Strange to have a word for something so secret

When the tyrant was safely asleep, Will asked me if I wanted to go to the field. I said no, let's go to bed

But Daisy

She's feeling better. Aren't you Daze?

She coughed, nodded

I don't know, said Will. Come to the

No. Look

I took Daisy by the hand and told her to get in bed with Pa if she was tired. But don't wake him up, I warned

Will frowned

Come on I hissed, and pulled him through the door

What if your father

Push the dresser against the door

I'm really not sure this is a good idea Alice. But he did what I told him

I took off my white dress. It lay on the floor like milk. We kissed, and we kissed, and

'Shall we rest here for a minute?'

We stand beside the roots of a thick, old oak tree. The air is warmer now, or perhaps it only feels so because we have been walking. The sky is hardly visible through the canopy above us, but the little I can see looks clouded and grey. I remember flashes of the words I read in my father's journal, but it is all so strange, so hard to understand, that I push it away. Later; I will think about it later. For now, I stand, eyes closed, and listen to the silence, the way our father taught us all to do. High up, the leaves are whispering, though down here there is barely a breath of air. The birds are quiet, or far away. Only one call splits the stillness: a harsh, repetitive *hoo-hee*. It sounds like a question to which the caller knows there can never be an answer. And yet it goes on asking, over and over: *hoo-hee? hoo-hee?*

'Anything wrong, Alice?'

I open my eyes and he is looking at me, his eyes narrowed.

'Are you feeling unwell or?'

'No. Just listening.'

There is a distance between us today which I have not felt since the beginning, since that first kiss. What is it that has set this huge mountain 'tween our hearts and tongues? It's the not knowing, I suppose: the event on the horizon, still invisible, at least to me. I begin to guess where we must be headed, but still I don't know why.

Hope, Hope, and, like a shadow issuing blackly from its heels, fear.

But if Will is truly leaving, if all this is his long good-bye, then we should not be as we are today. I do not wish my last memory of him to be so sad and estranged.

I think of all the questions I've never asked him – because I was too shy, because I feared the answers, because I felt there would always be time, later – and they prick me with regret.

I do not want him to go. I will not let him leave me behind. Whither thou goest, I will go. Where thou diest, will I die.

'Hold me, Will.' My voice comes out as small as Daisy's. And as childish, as needy.

Will smiles as though remembering something and moves toward me. I squeeze him with a sudden desperation.

'Gently, Alice,' he says. 'My ribs, remember?'

'Sorry,' I say. 'You can hold me though, can't you?' He does, and I feel so relieved. Tighter, I want to whisper, but soon, too soon, his muscles relax and I sense his mind is elsewhere. I look up at him. I see first the finger-shaped bruises on his neck, and then his face, turned upwards and away. He is staring into the distance, or perhaps only thinking.

'Come on,' he says, 'let's eat and have a rest. After that we've got to get going again.'

He takes a blanket from the rucksack and spreads it on the ground, near the roots of the oak. The two of us sit down. The sudden smell of wild mint: I must have crushed some with my hand. I look around and see a cage of trees, leaves, nettles, bracken, the odd bar of sunlight. Our hands touch

We kissed, and we kissed, and we

Bang bang bang

His tongue poised over me, warm air on my thighs, the wanting like a wound. Please please please

Just a minute said Will, to my father's rude knocking.

Knock knock knock who's there in the name of Beelzebub?

I laughed and whispered Please

Knock knock, never quiet

Open the fucking door yelled the tyrant

Just a minute

But we wouldn't couldn't have a minute longer, just a minute longer to

Bang Bang Bang

The pressure left my thighs and the bed sprang up beneath me as Will stood and began putting his clothes on. I looked across at my dress, my white dress, spilled over the floor. Like milk, I thought, and laughed again

The door moved

Stop laughing, Will hissed. What's wrong with you?

He threw the dress to me and I frowned, smiling, at his incomprehension

Open up or I'll fucking kill you

I stood up then, frightened, and quickly dressed. No underwear: my little invisible rebellion against the tyrant. His voice though . . . it was rawer, more rageful than I had ever heard it. I put my hand on Will's shoulder as he stood watching the door. Be careful, I said, suddenly afraid of what my father might do

He glanced back at me, over his shoulder. Stern and handsome. The slightest of nods

The door thundered again and he stood there, shaking, red-faced, wild-eyed, staring at us, mad as Lear

You did this you did this it was you who

'Aren't you hungry Alice?'

On the blanket are a bottle of water, a loaf of raisin bread, some goat cheese wrapped in fig leaves, and four apples. We eat and drink in silence. When I've eaten enough, I lay back against the tree's roots and close my eyes

I was in the bedroom, listening at the door. Outside the thunderstorm had moved off but the rain continued, relentless. We children had been sent to bed so that the men could talk. My body still itched with lust, my mind raced with images of how close we had been, that afternoon. And now the desire was mixed with fear. What was happening, in that room? I yearned to slip through the door, to listen at the threshold of the music room, but if my father found me, he might

And so, here I was, standing, knees bent, my ear to the keyhole, listening. I had been standing in this position for an hour or so, but their voices had been low and I had hardly caught a word. And then

The tyrant shouted so loud that I feared he would wake the spy

the hell gives you the right to

Then there was quieter muttering and again, drunk, enraged, the tyrant yelling

talk to me about morals when

then a few indistinct words, and

going to fucking calm down you patronising

Then it went quiet. Eerily quiet. I held my breath and tried to listen harder, but all I could hear was my own pulse, hard in my throat and ears

Oh God oh please don't let him hurt my Will

Soon after that, a door slammed and there was silence. Who had left? Will or my father? Or both? I listened, desperate to open the door and discover the truth. But some instinct held me back. Then I heard more noises, guttural, wordless, and then the outside door opened and closed again. So they were both gone. I waited a few seconds, then opened the door and slipped out into the corridor.

All was black but for a rhombus of blue light

XXVI

The words keep pouring out my mouth, I don't care how loud, I am dealing with the Devil here. The words keep pouring out my mouth as if God were speaking through me, the power of his wrath terrible to behold, and he puts his hand inside his shirt like he's been wounded. The words keep pouring out my mouth, growing louder and more righteous, like a hurricane roaring from deep in my chest and up through my throat and out my mouth, blowing him away, burning his face in God's wrath, and he takes his hand from inside his shirt and in it, trembling, is my pistol.

'Don't come any closer.'

I laugh. 'What are you going to do, boy? Kill me?'

'I will if I have to.'

I stare in his eyes, and take a step closer to the barrel of the gun.

'Move back, I'm warning you.'

I take another step closer.

'Get back or I'll . . .'

A third step. My chest is touching the end of the gun now. It shakes in his hand. I make a sudden motion with my hand to grab it, and he smashes the gun against my face.

Blinding pain, like fire. I stumble, fall to my knees.

I open my eyes and the walls and floor are red. He is gone. Something is dripping, hot and wet, onto my cheek.

I put my hand to the source of the fire, and feel ripped-up skin above my eyebrow. My hand comes back bloody. Eye for eye wound for wound burning for burning. I stand up and go out of the door, through the kitchen, out of the ark, into the thick, slashing rain. The sky is black and starless, the heavens turning a blind eye to this island. God leaving it all to me. Thunder rumbles, far off, and I listen to the silence that follows, hear his footsteps, his breathing, close by, and run in that direction, the fiery wheel in my mind stuck on FURY FURY FURY. I'm going to fucking kill you you fucking smell him I can smell him in the darkness in the rain fee fi fo fum I smell the blood of a Babylonian. Out I go by the vines but no he's not there so double back and round the side of the chicken shed. I stop. I can't see him but I can hear him breathing, panicked and ragged, beneath the RADTRADTRADTRADTRADT of the rain on the ark roof. Hiding from me. Afraid. I hold my breath and move, low down, stealthy, towards the *heehawhee-hawheehaw* of his breathing. Still it's too dark to see, and then. The neon flash of sheet lightning strobes the whole scene, and. There. There. I see him standing, his back to me, peering round the side of the chicken shed, looking for me. The world goes black again and I throw myself at where he stood. I haven't tackled like that since high school. An unmanly yelp escapes his mouth and he goes down with a soft crump, like the cat when I threw it against the tree trunk. But HE's not dead, O no, not yet. He's thrashing away beneath me, but I crawl over his body and pin his arms to the ground, digging my knee in the small of his back. 'Ugh,' he says. I check his hands: no gun. It musta spilt somewhere in the night somewhere on the ground. Never mind. There are other ways of killing. Vengeance is mine and I will repay, saith the Lord. I am Alpha and Omega, the first and the last, and the wages of sin is DEATH. I punch him in the side of the head a few times, my fists sliding off him in the rainslick, then stand up and kick him in the ribs. He flips over, tries to escape, and I bring my heel down on his nuts. Screaming, he tries to trip me with his hands but I just come crashing down on him, knees first, and hear the crack of a rib or two. He punches me in the mouth, and again on the eyebrow, where my wound stings like fucking fire. But the wasps are asleep: I am cool and collected. He thought he was stronger than me, but now. 'Get off me!' he cries, and lightning illuminates his face again: the terror, the pain. 'What do you want?' Fool, this night thy soul shall be required of thee. Thou camest in with vanity, and departest in darkness, and thy name shall be covered with darkness. 'Help me!' he shouts to the black night, but his voice is weak, the rain loud, the others all asleep. I straighten my arms, triceps tensed and bulging, feeling their still-immense strength, the power that comes from righteous FURY, and. There is no knowledge, no wisdom, no morality, nor love, in the grave, whither thou goest. And my hands, my vast ugly leatherskinned hands, tighten round his young slender throat, his lying contaminated poisonous throat, and. Fear God, and give glory to Him, boy, for the hour of His judgement is come.

XXVII

All was black but for a rhombus of blue light coming from the kitchen doorway. I moved through and opened the outside door. Lightning flared across the sky. I had a sudden bad feeling. Barefoot on the grass, my feet soon covered with mud, my nightdress soaked by rain, I ran around the side of the ark

Where were they? My heart was beating fast. Inside the bamboo hut? I ran there and found it empty. In the orchard? I ran past the vines and peered through the darkness. No sign of them there either. Then I heard a noise. The words were indistinct, but it sounded like Will's voice. It came from somewhere behind the chicken shed. Again I ran, terrified now at what I might discover, terrified that I might arrive too late

And there I found them, in a slick of mud, the two of them barely visible in the teeming darkness

My father was kneeling astride Will's body, his face so ugly in profile and rage that for a moment I didn't recognise him. All was still, tense, balanced; there was almost no noise at all now, apart from the rain. I stared at my father's deformed face, and then traced with my eyes the diagonal lines of his arms, those lines which led down inexorably from his shoulders, the two of them joining, meeting, in his thick forearms and large, coarse, oar-like hands, which were covering the delicate span of Will's throat. I screamed. My father looked around and instantly pulled his hands from Will's throat, as if it were fire

Alice, I

He looked down at his hands. As if they were actually burned

I, um. It's not what you think, I was

He sounded like he was talking in his sleep

Listen, Alice, you mustn't

But I was no longer Alice. A hellcat, a vengeful beast, I went for his ugly face with my nails, scratching and hitting. I could feel his stubble and the rain-greasy skin and the jawbone and cheekbone moving and something warm and liquid. I could smell his foul wine breath. I could hear his sleeper's moans. I could see nothing, nothing at all. I scratched and hit and kicked and bit and spat until he crawled away from Will's body, beyond the circle of mud, beyond my vision, and I put my hands softly to my true love's face

It's all right, Will said, in a small voice, then coughed, swallowed. He sat up and I cradled him. It's all right

He was shivering. The rain was pouring over us

Will I love you

Alice there's

Oh Will, oh Will, I was so frightened

Alice there's something I need . . . to tell you. Tomorrow

Yes, tomorrow. Tell me tomorrow. Come now

'I think it's time we were going.'

I open my eyes. The air is greyer, mistier than before. 'All right.'

I stand up and we begin to walk. Beneath our feet the ground has turned to rocks, mossy and cracked and shifting, so we must measure each step or risk a twisted ankle, a broken neck

You were strangling him

The words almost got stuck in my throat. The anger was blocking their way. I stared at my father, who stood the other side of the kitchen table. It was morning. The morning after. Yesterday morning

I

You would have killed him

I honestly

I will never forgive you

He shuddered. Alice I'm so sorry, I

His eyes were bloodshot and yellow-clouded; such feeble and desperate orbs that I could not look into them

Nothing you say can ever

Alice, you may not believe this, but I am sure that, even if you hadn't come, hadn't found us

You would have killed him. He would be dead

No, no, no, I don't believe that. I know it looked bad, looked terrible, but I think somewhere deep inside me that

Don't lie to me. I saw you

Something inside me would have screamed out No, would have stopped me from

The words froze in his throat, and I stared at him again. You're wasting your breath. I don't believe a word you say anymore

It was his turn to look away. Where is Will now?

I smiled. In my bed

He swallowed, nodded, stared at the table. At his hands, on the table. His large brutish strangler's hands

Has he told you

Told me what

He sighed. It doesn't matter. Listen, Alice, whatever happens, whatever anyone says, I love you, and always have and always will. And anything, everything I said and did, it was for your sake

He looked me in the eyes again, and I shook my head. In a gentler voice I said

I can never trust you again Pa

That's a shame, he said, his voice breaking. That's a terrible shame

We walk for an unguessable length of time, moving more and more slowly. Soon we cannot even see the ground below us. The mist is thickening and all is palest grey.

'Damn this cloud,' Will hisses, to himself.

'We could stop for a while. It might clear.'

'Yeah, you're right. There's no way I can tell where we're going like this. And these rocks are dangerous. Come on, let's find somewhere more open where we can sit down.'

We walk sideways, until the rocks below give way to stones, soil, creepers, weeds. Will uses his hands to ascertain the lie of the land. He kicks away brambles and nettles, and eventually finds a bed of broken ferns on which we can sit. He leans back against a tree and I lie with my head on his chest, too tired to read or think. All sound is muffled inside the cloud. The milky vapour seems to remove us from the world of conversations, of each other. Even touching, we are as alone as we are in dreams. Not like yesterday, when

what would your

We were in the lake, our legs and hands touching under the water. The air was so hot. I wanted to kiss him like

before, like all the other times, but the spy and the tyrant
were both close by, pretending to watch Daisy as she
splashed in the shallows. I whispered

Come with me

Where?

You know where

Oh

Will shot a brief look at my father, who was splashing
water at Daisy, trying to hide his fear as she laughed,
crouched down, jumped up. Trying so hard to make
everything seem normal

All right then. You go first Alice, I'll be there in a minute

I squeezed his hand and left the water. Without a glance
backwards, I walked through the trees to the other side.
There was no shade, but at least here I couldn't be seen.
My desire was baking, rising, growing in the vast endless
oven of the afternoon.

At the edge of the sunflowers I turned back to face the
way I had come. And there he was, a dark precise I on the
horizon. He was coming

Come in unto me

I got down on my knees and crawled through the
narrow gaps between the sunflowers. For once, the air
here was barely any cooler than the air beyond. I could
taste my own sweat in my mouth. I crawled to the middle
and took off my bikini. *But what would your* I lay on my
side in shadow, naked, listening to the grazed sound my
breath made as it left my lungs. And I waited

To wait, to wait, to

give me your will Will I want to swallow your pride I
want to taste a little honey at the end of your rod in mine
hand and now

I could hear him coming: a stifled cough, and the sound of his hands and knees on the dry ground. When at last he emerged into view I murmured

Will, come

Alice

dup me farce me tup me stanch me love me shove me lick me suck me fuck me

He crawled closer, I breathed his breaths, one, two, three times, and then. I attacked him: threw my face at his, pressed my lips hard against his mouth and flickered my tongue inside. I scratched his back he sucked my nipple I bit his shoulder he

A sound disturbs me. I open my eyes, but the mist is as thick as before. I close my eyes again and listen closely. The sound of twigs cracking, an animal breathing. I wonder what it is – if perhaps my father – but Will is here. I am not alone. I touch his thigh

His body stirred. Mine was burning, yearning. I whispered

Come in unto me

Hmm?

Come in unto me

He stopped kissing my neck and looked at me curiously

What do you mean?

It's what they say in the Bible

I was blushing

I don't know how else to say it

Oh. But

Please Will I love you I want you to

I want to Alice, but I can't. How can I? You're

Don't say I'm too young

I know I know but you are

I'm older than Juliet

Alice I can't what would your

I don't care what he thinks. I wish he were dead

What would your

I don't care I wish

What would your mother say?

Dub. Dub. Dub. The echoing pulse in my ears

My mother?

Alice I'm sorry I

Hope, Hope, and

My mother's dead

Your mother's alive Alice

But. Dub. Dub. Dub. Hope, Hope, and

Alice I'm really sorry I wanted to tell you before but it's been

My mother's alive?

She is. She wants to see you again. She sent me here

You know her but but she can't how can she

Hope, Hope, and, like a shadow issuing blackly from its heels, Fear

I know her well she's a wonderful woman she wants me to bring you all

But I don't understand how can she be? The sea, it

Your father lied to you about what happened to your mother, Alice. He lied to you about a lot of things. I've been wanting to tell you the truth ever since I arrived, but . . . I don't know. I went along with all he said because I needed to win his trust, to begin with. Then I needed to win *your* trust, and Finn and Daisy's. And after that, I kept saying to myself, today I'll tell her, but . . . it was your father's force of personality, his *will*. To go against it would have been like swimming into the tide, and it was so much easier to just let myself float. Especially as the current took me to such beautiful places

He stroked my face, and I touched his fingers to my lips. It's OK, I said, it doesn't matter

Anyway, I felt I had to warn your father first. It would have been better if he'd told you himself. Told all of you. I still don't know if Finn and Daisy will believe me over him. But so I warned him yesterday, after you'd gone to bed, and. Well, you saw what happened

Yes, I saw

I open my eyes. Is the mist clearing?

XXVIII

I can feel it, ghostlike, chilling my bones. I can feel it, in the white vapour of the cloud that envelops this forest. I can feel it, like a premonition of wintertime. The COLD.

The harvest is past, the summer is ended, and we are not saved.

It was after breakfast when I walked in and found Alice's bed empty, the sheets cold. O generation of vipers, who hath warned you to flee from the wrath to come? I told Finn to look after Daisy and ran up to the orchard. From the tallest cherry tree, my eyes scanned the horizon in every direction. The sea was markless, smooth as glass. There was no sign of them.

Have they already gone?

I reach the final slope and pause for breath. I can feel the wasps stirring in my chest. Easy, take it easy. I look up through the mist and see the birches and beeches disappearing upwards into whiteness, haggard and petrified, like the sinners of Babylon vainly waiting and praying to be let into Paradise. Will I even be able to see anything from the top of the Tree? Is it already too late? I shiver, and remember yesterday, sitting by the lake with Finn.

We were in shadow, side by side, watching Daisy splash in the kneehigh water. That was the day's only solace, seeing her so happy and unafraid in the lake, as if nothing had ever happened. I kept my eyes on her all the time. Why? Because I was scared she might go under again?

Yes . . . and no. It was also to stop Finn looking in my eyes and seeing the story of the night before writ there in letters of blood.

He asked about the wound over my eye, of course, and about the bruises on Will's face. I told him we'd had an accident, but I knew he didn't believe me. Even Daisy could feel the strangeness in the air. They'd probably overheard me pleading for Alice's forgiveness, my tears and Sorry I'm so fucking sorry what can I. So I wasn't fooling anybody. But I could hardly tell him the truth, could I?

We sat on the bank of the lake, watching Daisy and, beyond her, Alice and Will. Whenever Alice caught me looking at her, she stared back, cold and hateful, and the SHAME and REGRET soaked through me, so I tried not to let my eyes wander. I blanked out the black spinning horror of the world and filled my whole vision with Daisy's smile, her laughter, the sexless perfection of her little body, the light reflected onto her skin by the water. For truly the light is sweet, and a pleasant thing it is for the eyes to behold the sun.

But remember the days of darkness, for they shall be many.

The next time I looked up, they'd gone. Alice and Will. They weren't in the lake anymore. I wondered then if they were escaping, if he'd told her those LIES about her mother yet. I wondered if I would ever see my daughter again. But she came back without him in the evening and I thought everything that maybe everything was maybe everything would be.

Fuck it.

She is lost to me now, whatever I do.

I am as water spilt on the ground, which cannot be gathered up again. Let mine eyes run down with tears and let them not cease, for my whole fucking life is broken with a great breach, O with a very grievous blow.

I went in the cabin this morning, and found it gone. My journal. The story of the last ten years of our lives. I'd tried to burn the pages, but. Has she read it yet – what remains of it? Does she KNOW? The sky ought to crack open when she does. But if a tree falls in the forest with no one there to hear it, does it even make a noise?

XXIX

Is the mist clearing? Perhaps – it seems more luminous than before – but it is still too dense to walk through. And anyway Will has fallen asleep. I look at his bruised face tenderly, slumped backwards against the tree trunk, his mouth slightly open. The air is cold, so I zip his fleece up to his chin, and lightly kiss his cheek.

Feeling thirsty, I open the rucksack and hunt inside for the bottle of water. And see the black book. My father's journal. I forget my thirst and pick up the book.

I feel

I feel like I am about to open my eyes for the first time in my life. And I'm afraid of what I might see.

I let the book fall open by chance, and force myself to read.

. . . walked back down to where we'd left the truck. Suddenly I knew what I had to do. I removed all the bags from the back of the truck, then got in the cab and drove to the edge of the path. Killed the engine, left the stick in neutral and the handbrake off, and got out again. Briefly I looked down, over the edge, into a green abyss. Then I walked behind the truck and pushed. For ages, nothing happened, I was pushing and pushing, against like a solid wall, and then the wall slowly melted and moved away on its own, wheels turning, hood leaning, the whole weight tumbling over the edge and me standing there, dazed by vertigo, the thrill of it rushing thru me, watching our last link to the old world smash dreamily into the mountainside 1 . . . 2 . . . 3 times and finally explode in a tiny ball of flame, no bigger than the flare of a match, no louder than . . .

Will murmurs something in his sleep. For a moment I think he is going to wake. He doesn't, but it reminds me that time is short; soon the mist will clear and we will have to begin walking again. I turn a few pages and read on.

. . . to sleep soon. Christ my back and shoulders and arms ACHE. I look like I've got rocks under my skin. But I've nearly finished the fourth ladder now, and after that I'll just have to make the final platform and cut away some branches and I'll be able to see 360°. Like the bird's nest in a ship. That'll make me feel so much safer, being able to go up there every morning and check the horizon with the binoculars. I climbed up to the top branches yesterday evening and took a look and there was nothing – nothing at all as far as my eyes could see. For the moment I do believe we're safe. Nobody knows we're here. And yet . . . something still bothers me. I know what I have to do, and that'll be a hell of a job, but . . . once it's done, it'll be like we really are cut off from the world here. All alone . . .

. . . of the morning and Mary's just got out of bed. Daisy was crying when I came in, and I picked her up out of the cot, but my hands were so frozen and covered in dirt that she screamed even louder – and then Finn and Alice started fighting. Damn Mary, I'm out there all fucking day in blizzards and darkness, digging this endless fucking moat and she's got nothing to do but look after the kids, cook a few meals and keep feeding logs into the range and she can't even manage that without moaning. She started crying last night when the kids had gone to bed, saying it was so desolate here etc etc. Well what the fuck did she expect? It's winter up a mountain for Christ's sake! It's so tough staying patient with her, but I know I have to. I keep telling her that spring'll be here soon and how we're free from all the fears we had in the city, but . . .

Moat. My chest tightens as I read the word again. It is a word I remember from the Tales. But how. I glance at

Will's face – his closed eyelids twitching violently, as if he's remembering my father's attack – and then back at the half-burnt book.

. . . is killing me I swear! Still no rain. The sun's been out all day, so the snow's melted and at least Mary and Alice have cheered up a bit (they were out all afternoon planting potatoes – which we'll damn well need because we've got thru more than half the preserves already!) but FUCKING HELL how did I fuck up the calculations on how much water I'd need so TOTALLY? I've diverted the streamwater and shovelled all the goddamn snow into it but it's still not even half full. It looks so sad, so fucking ridiculous – just a gigantic damp ditch! I want to cry. Tho Finn made me laugh this evening when he started playing in it like it was a paddling pool. I had to tell him to come out because I was afraid he'd rip the liner. Oh please God let it rain tomorrow . . .

The further in I go, the more pages I skip each time, so that moons wax and wane, first slowly and then in a blur of speed, through my fingers.

. . . rain finally stopped sometime last night. It was weird, not hearing that snaredrum rattle on the roof for the first time in, what, a month? I hadn't even been outside for about a week, because the storm was so torrential. It wouldn't have surprised me if there really HAD been a flood, and that the whole world were drowned except us. But so I went out this morning, at first light – the sky white, the air fresh and warm – and walked around the gardens, checking all the plants. Most of them were dead of course, tho the saplings and potatoes are OK. Then I walked over to where I dumped all that sand, and . . . found myself looking out across an apparent infinity of water, reflecting and meeting the sky in an invisible line. The HORIZON. I stared at it in disbelief and euphoria for like an hour. Even now the thought of it makes me laugh with triumph. I've done it! I've built an ocean! An island at the end of the . . .

. . . love to Mary last night, but it didn't work. She was dry and then, when I was finally inside, she started crying again. I asked her what was wrong and she wouldn't speak, so we had another like hourlong Q&A at the end of which she finally confessed that she was depressed because she was dreading the coming winter. I mean Jesus fucking Christ it's the middle of the summer! The sky's permanently blue, the air's warm and smells like heaven, everything we've planted is in bloom, the children are happy . . . all's glorious. It's fucking wonderful, but Mary says she can't forget the 'horrors' of our first winter. God I love her – I <u>do</u> – but if she doesn't snap out of this soon, it's going to . . .

. . . fell asleep as the sun came up, with nothing resolved, and I kept the kids out of her way all morning so she could rest. When she woke, I thought, she would know what she was going to do. But she didn't. She was still as lost as ever. So finally I told her she had to make a decision: stay forever or go now. She nodded when I said this, looking almost relieved, but she didn't say anything else about it. I made dinner in the evening, and she sat with the kids in the fire room, hugging and kissing them. She sang them a lullaby at bedtime, and then she went to our room. I could hear her crying softly through the door. An hour or so later, she came to me and told me she'd made her decision. I didn't have to ask what . . .

. . . told her which path to follow, how to cross the valley and where to go after that. I would guess, if she can hitch a ride, that she'll be back in LA by tomorrow. She's got a loaded pistol in her bag, and more than $2000. I have no doubt she'll make it back safely. Whatever weaknesses she may have, if Mary truly wants something, she will walk through fire to get it. I know – I saw her give birth.

I hesitate to write this, but I must confess it crossed my mind at the last moment to end it, then and there. A gentle push is all it would've taken, and . . . well, if she ever changes her mind, if she ever breaks her promise, she knows our location – that's the trouble. That's what scares me. It gnaws at me already, the regret. A hand on her back, the abyss below, and all our fears would have been over. But I couldn't. I just couldn't . . .

. . . goodbye ceremony was nearly two months ago. Since then, we've had the daily silences and prayers for Ma, and a couple more rememberings. Only Alice weeps now. Finn's sad when he thinks about her, and sometimes he cries out in his sleep, but he's forgetting her already, I can tell. I sing songs and tell stories about her drowning in the sea, falling from the ark. Alice hated this to begin with, but tonight, for the first time, she didn't say a word, didn't argue. It's hard, of course, lying to your children – it makes me feel bad. But you can't live in paradise with the stains and burns of hell still clinging to you. You have to wash yourselves clean, to grow a new skin – you have to bathe in the waters of Lethe. And in a year or two, I believe, perhaps even Alice will . . .

. . . drunk and I can't stop crying Ive been crying all damn night it was so good this evening I roasted a chicken for the moonday feast and we ate it with green beans and potatoes from our gardens and god it tasted so good! Three years we've been here now. <u>Three years</u>! Mary died nearly two years ago and we still sing and talk about her everyday. Shes a heroine now a legend she should be grateful. So we sat round the table watching the sunset over the Afterwoods God it was so BEAUTIFUL and then we sang I played the guitar and Alice played Morning Has Broken on the violin I was so proud of her I hugged her tight and I read em a fairytale at bedtime – Alice still likes hearing em even if shes read em all herself and now shes started reading the bible shes so clever such a smart girl. And but I read the story and kissed em goodnight and I was about to leave when she called me back and said 'I miss Ma'. So do I honey, I said. 'I wish she werent dead' she said. And jesus the GUILT but theres no reason no reason I only told em those stories to make their lives better safer freer more beautiful I swear . . .

As I turn more pages, something falls from the book into my lap. I pick it up – a piece of paper, half-burnt.

It is filled with a different handwriting, the letters larger and rounder than my father's, and it begins with the words 'My darling children'. Instantly I scan the bottom of the letter for the signature and there see the word that stops my heart: 'Mom'.

Inbetween it says:

This is the hardest letter I've ever . . .
I'm not good with words so I'm s . . .
you all how much I love . . .

I'm leaveing because I can't . . .
can't. I wish I could take you w . . .
would be selfish and unfare of . . .
and I know he's right, you all . . .
of the fresh air, country side etc . . .
what else to say.

I've promissed I will nev . . .
you but I hope maybe one . . .
show you how much I lo . . .

Be good for your . . .
remember me.

With all my . . .

'Alice?' I look up from the book, and Will is staring at me, his face gentle, concerned. 'Are you all right?'

I nod, and he wipes the tears from my cheeks. I look down at my hands, which are stained black from the burnt edges of the paper.

'She promised your father she wouldn't do anything to
. . . but she missed you all so . . . in the end it was . . .'

'Later,' I whisper. 'Tell me later. Not now.'

I put my head on Will's shoulder and he holds me.

'It looks like the mist is clearing,' he says. 'Do you feel
ready to go on?'

'Yes,' I say. 'Yes, I'm ready.'

XXX

Up the last slope I go, holding on to low branches as I climb, twigs cracking under my feet. The mist is clearing now. Thin wisps of it break up and dissolve as I move through. I reach the plateau and pause again, then walk between the redwoods until I am standing by the great tortured roots of the Tree of Knowledge. There I rest for a moment, looking up as high as I can. This ancient being whose head is pure wisdom, even she begins in earth, all dark and twisted and desperately clawing, like the men who seek to climb her. I see the boughs tremble in a gust of wind. At least, up there, I will know the truth. If they have fled the island, I will see them. And then I can.

And then I can what?

Follow them?

Forget them?

Kill them?

I don't know I don't know but I at least I will I suppose I if nothing else I will KNOW. (Sometimes it is better not to.)

I climb the ladder, pausing for breath at each platform. I do not look down. When I reach the top I lie flat on the platform for a while, breathing in and out, in and out, in and out, and counting my pulse as it slows.

And I shall know the truth, and the truth shall make me free.

I touch the field glasses to my eyes and look east, west, south, north. Nothing but the blank circling horizon, the sky and reflecting sea. The endless, waveless blue.

I sigh. So they have not gone. But in that case where are.

I hear something and hold my breath.

'Don't look down.'

It's HIM. Talking to HER.

Why is he bringing her here? How dare they come to this sacred, forbidden place? But of the Tree which is in the midst of the garden, I have said, Ye shall not climb it, neither shall ye look from it, lest ye DIE. But the serpent said to my daughter, Ye shall NOT surely die. For your father doth know that in the day ye look from this Tree, then your eyes shall be opened, and ye shall KNOW.

And I shall know the truth, and the truth shall make me mad.

Her head appears through the hole in the platform and I hide behind a branch. She walks to the edge of the platform and looks down, out, across. She sees. She knows.

Behold, the girl is become as one of us.

XXXI

The trees, ever taller, lean into the hill. They grow so close together here that we are able to pull ourselves up on their branches and trunks. Halfway up the slope we rest for a moment, both of us breathing hard, and I look up to the sky and see only a high ceiling of leaves. The mist has cleared, and we are nearly there

damn Mary digging this endless fucking moat as if there really had been a flood I've built an ocean an island at the end of love to Mary the children are happy but Mary says God I love her I love her but she sang them a lullaby crying softly her decision if Mary truly wants something she will walk through fire a hand on her back the abyss below only Alice weeps lying to your children I was so proud of her I hugged her tight lying to your children shes so clever such a smart girl I wish she werent dead wish I could take you all with me lying to your children to make their lives better safer freer more beautiful lying

'Steady, Alice.' His hand gently crushes mine. 'One more step.'

The ground beneath our feet falls away. I look down, puzzled, afraid, and discover that the earth is flat. Instead of rocks and roots, there is grass, dry leaves. The air is cool and silverish, and smells of lemons. The spaces between the trees are vast and the trees themselves are higher, grander than any trees I have ever imagined. The turmoil in my head is silenced for a moment.

'They're redwoods,' says Will. 'More than a thousand years old.'

He takes my hand, and we walk through the golden spaces. It is like a palace, this hilltop, the trees as pillars holding up the firmament.

We come to a tree so magnificently huge, you could lose yourself in the tangling folds of its roots. 'This is it,' says Will. 'The Knowing Tree that your father told you about.'

I look up its trunk, which climbs smoothly, branchlessly, higher than the top of our pine, and then continues way beyond that, almost to the point of invisibility.

'But I can't . . . I can't climb that.'

Will takes me by the hand and leads me round to the other side of the tree. 'Look.'

There is a ladder – like the one next to the wine barrel, but ten times longer – nailed to the trunk of the tree. I crane my neck. At the top of the ladder is a platform and, from there, another ladder leads even higher up the tree . . . to another platform.

'Don't be scared, Alice. You go first. I'll come up behind you, just in case.'

I swallow.

'You'll be fine, honestly. And the view is worth it, I promise.'

The view?

I put my hands on the first rung. They are so drenched with sweat, the wood feels like a snake's body slipping and squirming through their grip.

I count the rungs as I go. The numbers, big and simple, fill my mind, pushing away all hopes and fears, all day-dreams and distractions, all memories and premonitions.

The first ladder has forty-eight rungs. I emerge through the hole in the platform and stand upon it, holding the trunk like I must have held Pa when I was a little girl, when I loved him and this island was the world to me. Clinging to him. While he lied to me.

The second ladder has forty-two rungs.

Strangely, the higher I go, the less frightened I feel. The ground is so far below now, I sense I would have time to die and be transformed into a bird before I even hit the bottom.

The third ladder has forty rungs.

The view on the third platform is obscured by branches and leaves. There is no sense of elevation at all.

The fourth ladder has forty rungs.

As I stand on the fourth platform, I think of Finn and Daisy, my brother and sister, both of them down there, somewhere below me. I remember their faces, moments together. And then I think of my father. The tyrant. The liar. Pa. I can feel nails being hammered into my stomach.

I feel

I feel as though something precious has been stolen from my life, and I am about to steal it back.

I look at the cluster of bright leaves that surrounds me and remember my mother. Mom. The pictures of her in my mind are so much briefer, more faded and elusive, than those of my brother and sister and father. She is less real to me. And yet she is the one I dream of, yearn for, believe in. I would discard them all for her. In spite of her decision. In spite of my guilt. In spite of the nails in my stomach.

'One more ladder to go.'

I nod, and begin to climb.

The final ladder has thirty-nine rungs.

When I reach the top, I hear Will's voice call out, 'Don't look down.' He sounds like he's a long way below.

I emerge through a platform, larger than the others, in the crown of the tree. The platform is square, and has a barrier running around it so you can stand and look out, down, across in each direction. The branches have been cut so the view is clear. I stand up, and walk to the edge. What I see changes everything. My whole life. The whole world.

The sea is not a sea. The island is not an island.

I shudder, reeling from the shock – and the glory.

A shadow moves across the platform. I turn, expecting to see Will, and

XXXII

In the gentle heat of these gloaming rays, it's tough to believe I could feel the winter in my bones just a few hours ago. Could see the darkness of Doomsday approaching. Premature premonitions. O Lord I am sorry I ever doubted You.

I pour another glass, the wine seethrough, aglow, redshadowing in the late sunlight, and shout for Finn and Daisy again. I'm sitting under the branch roof, halfway down my second bottle, and the morning's mists are gone and forgotten. Less than a memory now, along with the morning's fear.

They've gone. They had to go. It was inevitable.

The harvest is past, but the summer is not ended, and we are saved.

'Finn!' I yell. 'Daisy!'

I try to keep the impatience out of my voice. Damn kids, where are they? The smallest flash of panic in my chest, and then I hear their voices from the other side of the ark, and see Goldie chasing through the grass. He stops, grabs a stick in his jaws, and turns to run back the way he came.

'Gold!' I shout. 'Come here, boy.'

The slightest hesitation, and then Goldie ambles towards me, panting, cautious, the stick held tight between his teeth. His eyes are pools of black. They search behind and around me, sad and full of longing. 'He's gone, Gold, it's no good looking for him. He's gone and he's never coming back.'

I rub the dog's head and he drops the stick, wet with drool, on my lap. I laugh. 'Who's your master now, hey, Goldie? Who's your master now?'

Woof.

'Yeah, that's right, boy. I am the First and Last.' I squeeze his head between my hands and stare hard into those sad black eyes. And I whisper: 'You ever betray me again, you son of a bitch, and you'll be gone too. You understand?' The dog whimpers, tries to retreat. I loosen my grip and rub his head again, smile. 'All right, you understand. I can tell. Don't worry, Goldie, everything's going to be fine now.'

A moment later, Finn and Daisy come round the side of the ark, both of them red-cheeked and smiling. 'There you are, Goldie,' shouts Daisy, and runs towards him. She strokes and hugs the dog, then looks up at me and smiles. 'We've been playing Fetch.'

'So I saw. You too, Finn?'

My son, embarrassed by his childish happiness, tries to bury the smile on his face, but traces of it remain, unhide-able. He frowns, 'Yeah.'

I pick up the glass and pour more wine into my mouth. It's soft and blackberryish on my tongue. And it dulls the dread, numbs the pain, turns the past to mere specks of dust seen in the slanting rays of sunset.

Just dust.

'Pa, where are Will and Alice?'

I shrug. 'No idea, Finn. Anyway, what shall we eat for supper?'

Briefly, while we eat, I look in Finn's eyes.

'Don't you think it's strange they're not here, Pa?'

One woe is past; and behold, there come two more woes hereafter.

'No, I'm sure they'll turn up soon.'

I look down at the food on my plate, and I know what I have to do. When I've swallowed the last mouthful, I look up and say, 'Time for bed, children.'

'But it's still light, Pa.'

'What about Alice?'

I sigh through my nose. 'Finn. Daisy. Don't make me get mad. It's Time For Bed, all right?'

I tuck them in and kiss them goodnight, as I've always done, but tonight they are wide awake and insatiable, asking questions the way baby birds demand food. To calm them, I hang a dark cloth over the porthole and tell them to read by candlelight. But still the same damned questions keep repeating.

Where's Alice?

When is she coming back?

Why isn't she here?

What is she doing?

I begin to sweat in the airless little room. Finally I snap and say I don't think she's coming home tonight, and they look at me, both, with saucer eyes. It's the first time they've gone to sleep without their sister and they're frightened, I guess. Or maybe excited, I can't tell.

They're silent anyhow, so I kiss them each once more on the forehead and say goodnight, warning them in the doorway to blow out their candles before they fall asleep.

'Finn, you're in charge,' I say, and he nods sombrely.

'Pa?' he says, as I close the door. But there is no time.

'Night, Finn,' I bellow, and move quickly through the kitchen, and outside.

I lock the door of the ark.

To the west the sky has turned orange and red over the silhouetted Afterwoods. I need to run or it will be dark before I get there. I need to run or it will be too late. I could wait till dawn, of course, but the urgency, the gravity, the towering importance of my task eats away at me. It gnaws my guts – the ANGER, the REGRET – and I sprint up through the orchard, past the cornfield, along the side of the lake, till I come to the forest's edge. And enter.

Instantly I'm in the bluegreen murk of twilight, but I don't slow down. *They must never.* The continuing existence of the thing seems suddenly like the most gigantic and dangerous oversight of my life. How could I leave it there, that invitation to chaos, that vertical pathway of evil, after what happened this morning? To witness its effects, and yet to let it remain. What was I thinking of?

I go to the cabin and pick up the chainsaw, the bottle of gasoline, then carry them, as fast as I can, up the hill. I rest before the final slope, muttering 'Calm, calm down' between huge wheezing breaths. The wasps are flying, my eyelids are flickering, but I can't stop it will be too late unless. Wearily I heave my twin burdens from tree to tree, until the birches and beeches are below me and only the great redwoods lie ahead.

I walk, the chainsaw's teeth dragging in the dirt, and eventually drop it and the gas bottle before the roots of my enemy. Like gauntlets. Yes, my enemy, all the time my enemy, and I never knew. Never understood. I look up at it, this massive rebuke, this brazen traitor, and whisper, 'No more.'

No more will you lead them on, no more will you steal my children, O Tree of Knowledge. One woe is past, but two more come hereafter. I must nip the devil in the bud I must cut him off at the roots I must saw his fucking soul in two to save my innocents, my flesh and blood, who sleep and dream while I, I stand here in shrinking light in spreading shadow and pour the gasoline into the hole, seal it up and pull the chain that spins the blades, grazes the air, sinks metal teeth into the devil's body.

They must never ever

Dust, clouds of dust, everywhere, blinding my eyes, filling my mouth, sticking to my skin, like the Past. The saw eats and eats the devil's body and the Past swirls all over and around me.

I am dead on my feet when I hear its mighty groaning and see the sky darken above me. They've gone they had to go it was inevitable. Sorry I'm so fucking sorry what do you want me to. For He will swallow up death in victory and wipe away tears from all faces. And there shall be no more death, neither sorrow, nor crying. Neither shall there be any more pain.

XXXIII

Soon as I breath in I no. The airs not warm on my I-lids like befor its cold an sower the menting grapes mixt up with erth an compost an woodsmells all sad from the spitting rain. I no shure as I no my names Finn an Ive got a hunerd an ten moons. Shure as I no Snowys dead an ahm fear full an lone some. Shure as I no theres no thing you can ever truely no I no summers ending. I curl up under the blankets to keep warm an let all the air out my lungs in a long low sigh. Winters coming I grieve in my head. Then I breath in a gen.

I sit up an open my eyes an I can see the grey light coming thru the gap in the doorway. The black bird in my chest flaps its wings. Gritting my teeth to gether I crawl out from the warm an climb down the bunk ladder. Daisys wheezing slowly so I no shes still a sleep but Alices beds emty she dint come home last night. Ahm fraid shell never come home a gen.

I put on my fleece an jeans an socks an trainers shivring in the chill air an walk thru to the kitchen. The ranges gon out I can feel the metals cold an theres no thing on the table. No eggs nor milk nor pancakes. Pa must still be a sleep. I go to his door an listen an there it is the roring crowking slobring noise he makes wen hes drunk too much wine the night befor. Some times wen I hear that I feel fret full an gret full but right now ahm jus leaved. I wer fraid hed maybe vanisht too like

Will an Alice. That me an Daisy wer all a lone on the I-land.

I think bout clecting some eggs but with the range out I cunt cook em any way an ahm too tired an low to go out an milk the goats so I serch with my hands in the cuberd till I touch some old weat cakes and dry figs an I take em out. I dremt that Snowy wer a live las night but wen I woke this morning I memberd he wernt an that sad nesses still fecting me now. I eat the cakes an figs at the table lissning to the rain fall on the roof. It sounds like Gods crying soft an lent less cus hes lernd he dont zist hes jus a lusion an the worlds only flesh an erth an water it dont mean any thing. I stare at the dark shapes in the wood table as I eat. An then Daisy comes in the kitchen.

Wats up Finn she asks.

No thing.

She looks round the kitchen thru sleepy eyes an I say The ranges out.

Wheres Pa.

A sleep.

Cant you light it.

I spose so.

Well you do that an clect the eggs an ahl go an get some milk.

Then shes gon out into the rain so I find a lighter an some kindling an logs an I get the range go-ing. Soon as its lit I feel better an I warm my hands over it. Then I member the eggs so I walk out to the shed an let the chickens out. The chicks are all grown up theyre as beady an grobbling as the old ones now. I clect the eggs. Theres only seven but its a nuff for the three of us I spose. I stare out thru the misty rain an see the rising all blurd tween sea an sky. Theyve gon all ready. Over the edge of the world. I carry the eggs back in the hollow in my fleece.

In the kitchen I put the eggs to boil an push my chair close to the range drying my hair an hands an face an warming my chilld bones. Daisy comes in with Goldy an a jug of milk. Theyre both soakt. Goldy shakes his fur so drops spray all over us but Daisys skins I-scold. I tell her to sit in my chair by the range wile I get her a towel from the cuberd then I help dry her hair an she sits there shivring an giggling an ahm real glad shes here that shes not gon like the others.

Do you think theyll come back I say not looking at Daisy as I crack the eggs head an peel the shell off to veal the wite under neath.

Who she says.

Will an Alice.

I dont no. Whereve they gon.

I dont no.

She shrugs like theres no thing mor to say an hits the spoon bottom genst her egg shell. We eat some egg the yokes like golden blood.

Wats that noise Daisy says after a wile.

I listen.

I can hear the rain on the roof an the flames in the range an Goldys rough breathing an some thing else I cant tell wat it is. I frown trying to member wat the sound minds me of. Then it comes to me. It minds me of me the day Pa found me by Snowys grave stone. Me sobbing. Crying so hard it felt like my heart wer go-ing to come up out my throat. But ahm not sobbing now an neithers Daisy. An Will an Alice arent here.

Its Pa says Daisy.

Pas a sleep I ply.

Maybe he woke up.

But it cant be Pa he only cries in the evenings wen hes drunk wen hes not him self. Hes strong in the mornings. Hes normal in the mornings. He is. I tell my self all this not Daisy an I watch as she stands up.

Come on she says.

It cant be I want to say it cant be Pa but I can hear him louder now that choking sobbing retching like a lil boy but real deep an loud an rong sounding.

Come on Daisy peats.

I get up from my chair an follow her out the kitchen an thru the hall. The two of us stand outside Pas door lissning. Then Daisy nocks.

Pa.

Silents. Sobbing.

She nocks a gen an says his name but the same thing happens. So Daisy opens the door an goes in. I follow her and see Pa neeling on his bed his head in his hands his shoulders go-ing up an down in time with the sobbing whiches louder now realy loud an I feel sunly sick. Wats gon rong. I stand an stare at him too fraid to move or speak. The black birds flapping inside me. Some thing real bad musta happend. Some thing musta ript that can never be mended.

Thru blurd eyes I watch Daisy neel next to him on the bed and put her lil hand on his back an gin to rub. I wait for Pa to yell or push her a way but he dont. I watch her crouch an whisper some thing in his ear and his shoulders go-ing up an down. An then his shoulders go-ing up an down lessn they wer befor. An then an then his shoulders not go-ing up and down any mor an I listen to his sobs turning slowly into silents an I can hear wat Daisys whispring in his ear.

There there shes saying. There there. Dont cry Pa it wer jus a bad dream. Evry things go-ing to be all right. This is the bad part of the story but its go-ing to get better you no it is. Weare all go-ing to live haply

Everafter.